BLOOD BROTHERS

BLOOD BROTHERS

COLLEEN NELSON

DUNDURN
TORONTO

Editor: Carrie Gleason
Copy editor: Catherine Dorton
Design: Jennifer Gallinger
Cover design and composite image: Laura Boyle
Red spray paint: © istockphoto.com/skodonnell
Parking lot wall: © 123RF.com/donatas1205
Printer: Webcom

Library and Archives Canada Cataloguing in Publication

Nelson, Colleen, author
      Blood brothers / Colleen Nelson.

Issued in print and electronic formats.
ISBN 978-1-4597-3746-4 (paperback).--ISBN 978-1-4597-3747-1 (pdf).--
ISBN 978-1-4597-3748-8 (epub)

    I. Title.

PS8627.E555B56 2017   jC813'.6   C2016-903875-0
                                                 C2016-903876-9

1 2 3 4 5   21 20 19 18 17

Conseil des Arts du Canada   Canada Council for the Arts   Canada   ONTARIO ARTS COUNCIL CONSEIL DES ARTS DE L'ONTARIO an Ontario government agency un organisme du gouvernement de l'Ontario

We acknowledge the support of the **Canada Council for the Arts** and the **Ontario Arts Council** for our publishing program. We also acknowledge the financial support of the **Government of Canada** through the **Canada Book Fund** and **Livres Canada Books**, and the **Government of Ontario** through the **Ontario Book Publishing Tax Credit** and the **Ontario Media Development Corporation**.

Care has been taken to trace the ownership of copyright material used in this book. The author and the publisher welcome any information enabling them to rectify any references or credits in subsequent editions.

— *J. Kirk Howard, President*

VISIT US AT

  dundurn.com | @dundurnpress | dundurnpress | dundurnpress

Dundurn
3 Church Street, Suite 500
Toronto, Ontario, Canada
M5E 1M2

For James and Thomas,
who will always have each other

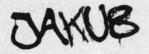

JAKUB

The sky gets pink close to dawn. Night bleeds away as the sun breathes life into day.

My finger throbs. The tip of it numb and sticky with paint. The street lamps flicker off as I stand back to survey my night's work.

Huge swoops of colour light up the background, like my tag has landed in a puddle of rainbow slime. "Morf," my other self, glows in bubble letters meant to look like liquid metal. All graff writers have a handle. Mine means something. To change, to morph. To become something else: a metamorphosis.

With a satisfied sigh, I turn my back on the side of the building and stuff spray cans, my bandana, and black book into my backpack. Hidden in shadows, I scale down the fire escape and drop to the alley, the cans in my pack rattling. In a few hours, people walking to the bus will look up and see my name flash before them.

It wasn't there yesterday. They'd never even noticed that building before. But, now, my name slaps them in the face. They can't ignore me. My name looms above, stomping on them.

Two guys stumble out of a house party. I watch as they try to open the latch on the chain-link gate. Too many fumbling fingers. They'll be trapped in the yard till their vision clears, or they pass out.

The rooming house rises up between two empty lots. The city tore down one house a few years ago and the other burned to the ground. Arson, the cops said. I smelled the smoke in my dream. Dad yelled at me to wake up as he tried to scoop me up, like he still had the strength to carry me. We made it out and watched from across the street, huddled in a blanket as flames engulfed the building. Two people died in the fire and I had nightmares for weeks.

There's two cop cars, their lights flashing, in front of the rooming house. The blue and red orb spins, reflecting off the windows. Shrugging off my backpack, I ditch it in the empty lot next door. I know they aren't there for me, but my heart pounds anyway. I swear and kick at a stone. If the sirens wake up my dad, he'll see I'm not asleep on the couch where I'm supposed to be.

Without my backpack, I feel naked, exposed. It's like battle armour. I eye the cops; a couple of them mill around the front yard, blocking my entrance. No police tape is up yet. That's a good sign. Means no one is dead. One of them looks at me, doesn't bother to question why I'm returning home at this time of the night. I was ready with an excuse if he had: I fell asleep at my best friend Lincoln's house.

I put my head down and brush past them, taking the steps in two strides. Two more cops stand outside 1D. The McLarens. Mr. and Mrs. Domestic Abuse. Should have guessed.

I cried angry tears the first night we moved to this place. When the landlady, Laureen, opened the door to the apartment, Dad and I froze in the hallway; neither one of us wanted to walk inside. It stank. Like piss and body odour. Laureen had promised to have it cleaned before we moved in. But she couldn't do anything about the stains on the floor or the foam exploding from the couch cushions. Dad explained why we were moving from our two-bedroom apartment to the rooming house. There was no choice. They raised the rent and he couldn't afford it anymore, not even with a housing subsidy. If we wanted a roof over our heads, this was it.

Laureen gave Dad two keys, held together by a red twist tie. He gulped and stuffed them in his pocket like he didn't want to admit they belonged to him. I knew what Dad was thinking, what he was always thinking. This wasn't the life he moved here for. We'd be better off in Poland than living in this shithole. But, he made his choice twenty years ago, promising my mom a life in Canada. They'd escaped under a barbed wire fence and hid in the trunk of a car, then relied on the kindness of strangers. And for what? So my mom could die after giving birth to me and Dad could end up with a mangled leg from his job at the train yard.

He could feel sorry for himself, but he doesn't. Polish pride, he calls it. There are some things that are non-negotiable: church every Sunday, good grades, and good food. No matter how tight things are, Dad always has a meal ready for me. I come home from school to find him limping between the sink and stove, boiling potatoes or stirring soup. My brain needs food, he says. We won't have empty stomachs. That was one thing we'll never have, empty stomachs. He had enough of that in Poland. A boy can't grow or succeed in school with hunger pains to distract him.

He probably should have been a chef. He hums to himself, old Polish folk tunes, when he cooks, his fingers turning crimson with beet juice. Or love songs, if he's feeling nostalgic, glancing up at the one photo we have of my mom. Grainy and out of focus, she's standing in front of the church, the golden spire rising from a white dome, a mosaic of the holy family glinting in the sun. Scrawny legs, made scrawnier by the fullness of her skirt, and bushy curls obscuring most of her face.

Father Dominic stopped by the apartment soon after we moved in. Taking a look around, he skimmed over the books and his eyes came to rest on the crucifix perched above the couch. He nodded at it, like he was greeting a friend. Father Dominic had baptized me and stood over my mother in the hospital as she took her last breath. All in the same week. It was touch and go with me in those early days. No one knew if I'd make it or not. I don't ask a lot of questions about what happened. Dad doesn't like to talk about it. Says I'm a blessing from God, no matter what. But then he gets teary and quiet.

The door clicks shut behind me. I half expect Dad to be sitting up waiting for me. But he's a heavy sleeper. Sirens in the night are so common, we've both learned to sleep through them. His snores fill the apartment, a low rumbly wheeze.

I pull back the sheet and blanket on the couch, leaving my jacket on the armrest. Closing my eyes, I picture the newly marked building. Like a baptism, I christened it mine.

I'll walk past it in the morning, to see how the colours look in daylight. I drift off to sleep content. I accomplished something this night. No one could accuse me of not leaving my mark on the world. It was there, for all to see.

LINCOLN

Henry has his feet up on the table in front of the TV like he never left, like he hasn't been in prison for the last eighteen months.

The door, a flimsy metal screen one, rattles shut behind me. I stare at him for a few minutes, trying to figure out if I'm supposed to be pissed, or happy to see him.

He doesn't say nothing either. His thick lips turn down in a frown. With eyes hooded like he's half-asleep, it's hard to tell what my brother's thinking.

I take a few more steps into the living room. "Hey," I start.

He stands up and growls. Prison made him bigger, more muscly. His shoulders start under his ears, rolling with bulges. New ink, a dagger dripping with red blood, is engraved in his neck. The gang tattoo for Red Bloodz. I take a step back, but in a second, he has his arm around my neck, squeezing it so hard I can't breathe.

I slap at it, but his forearm is like an iron bar. I'm a scrawny weakling compared to him. When I stamp my foot hard on his toe, he finally lets me go with a laugh. "Good to see you, bro." He takes my face in his hands and I scowl, like, *What the hell are you doing?* but he ignores it and pats the back of my head, jamming it into his chest. "God, it's good to be back."

He fills up the room. Takes it over with his size and gravelly voice.

"When'd you get back?" I ask, but what I mean is, *When'd you get out?* How long was he hanging with friends before he decided to put his feet up on our coffee table?

He gives an exaggerated shrug and sits back down on the couch. Right in the middle and stretches his arms out on either side, like he owns it. "Couple days ago. Fill me in, what's been going on around here?"

I pull my cap down low over my eyes and shrug. "I dunno. Nothing. The same."

"Who are you hanging with?"

"Koob."

"The Polish kid." He gives a snort, like it's not the answer he wanted. "Going to school?"

I nod. I go because Jakub goes. I'm not smart like him, but he helps me with homework and gives me the answers on tests.

"And?" He raises his eyebrows, like there should be more. "What? You're an angel? You got nothing else? Shit, man. You're dragging down the family rep."

Henry's twenty-one now. At my age, he'd been in and out of juvie for car thefts, vandalism, B and E.

I scratch my head, wishing for a second that I was a badass, just to have something to tell him. I could make something up, but Koob's always saying what a shitty liar I am. "Me and Koob paint, you know, not just tags, but like real good stuff."

"Oh yeah?" He picks up the remote and flicks through some channels. "Anything still running?"

"There's a piece up by that old cement factory. It's been up for a while." The sounds of a crowd cheering at an Ultimate Fighting Championship drown me out. He doesn't look at me.

Through the back window, I can see my five-year-old brother, Dustin, kicking a ball against the fence. Probably driving the neighbours crazy. Mom and Dad are sitting on lawn chairs with a beer and a smoke in each hand. A coffee tin between them over-flows with butts.

Guess they've seen Henry's back. Maybe they're outside celebrating. Not.

The last time Henry paid us a surprise visit, he got into it with Dad. They had a big fight. Cops got called. I went to Koob's, took Dustin with me, too. When we came home, there were a bunch of holes punched in the walls and we had to get a new TV. The old one sat outside on the curb for weeks cuz the garbage trucks wouldn't take it. Finally, someone smashed it and dumped it on the road. Then it had to get cleaned up.

I sit down on the couch. It sags in the middle — one of the legs is busted — so without wanting to, I lean toward him.

He puts a meaty hand on the back of my neck. "It's good to see you, Link. I mean it."

And I want to believe him so bad, it makes me sick.

"What's there to eat around here?"

"You want a menu?"

He gives me a sharp look. The corner of his mouth turns down.

"Joking," I breathe.

"I want some friggin' food, is what I want." He nods to Mom and Dad. "What have they been up to?"

"The same." I shrug. "Dad's been working road crew most of the summer." He comes home smelling like hot asphalt. His workboots stay outside. Mom doesn't want them in the house. "Auntie Charity and her kids came down from the rez for a while." For two weeks, I'd had to share my bed with a two-year-old who pissed it in the night. I was so glad when they left. "Mom took some classes at the alternative school." She took it real serious at first. Made us all leave the house so she could study and told Auntie Val she couldn't go to Fenty's Bar on weeknights any more.

"What happened?"

"Dropped out. Didn't like the teacher, or something."

Henry snorts like he isn't surprised Mom didn't stick with it. You're the one who's been in jail, I want to say. But don't.

"Yeah, well. I'm back now." He narrows his eyes, like he's got a plan. Like I need the help.

I do okay without you, I want to say.

"How old are you now?" he asks.

"Fifteen," I say. He snorts and I don't know if it's a good thing or a bad thing.

He pulls a phone out of his pocket and checks it. "Some friends are coming around. You wanna ride with us?"

I don't say anything cuz I don't know if he's serious or not.

"You got something else going on?" he asks, sarcastic.

I shake my head. I look at his arms, thick with muscles I'll never have, and the tattoo on his neck. My stomach flips and I tug the brim of my hat lower so he can't see me blinking. It's a nervous tick and makes me a crappy card player.

"I got nothing going on."

"Fuckin' A." He takes a breath and looks around. "It's good to be home."

I snort in agreement and lean back into the couch. The UFC fight is lopsided. One guy pummels the other one. I cringe when a roundhouse kick catches him in the jaw. Blood spatters the mat and the crowd roars. He goes for a body shot and the guy doubles over and then falls down.

"Get up, you pussy," Henry mutters at the TV.

"You back for good?" I ask.

Henry gives me a long look. "We'll see."

Outside, a black car with tinted windows pulls up and honks. Henry stands up. "You coming?"

I'm looking at the TV. The UFC guy is on the mat. Blood leaks out of his mouth and nose. He's lying on the mat like he's dead. The ref calls it. Angry jeers from the crowd follow me out the door. Nobody likes a loser.

Henry holds the neck of his tank top down so I can see his other tattoo. "Brothers to the End" is inked in fancy handwriting across his chest.

It's right there for everyone to see, dug into his skin with needles and ink.

"What do you think?" he asks. I don't think anything except it must have hurt.

"Got it inside for you and Dustin. I'm out now. I want things to be different."

We didn't even know he'd gone in till some girl came by. Said she was his girlfriend, had a ring and everything. Told Mom she was going up for a visit and did we want to send him anything? Mom and Dad fought that night. Dustin crawled into bed with me and I let him. I showed him how to hold a pillow over his ears and count as high as he could till it stopped. He fell asleep before it was over. In the morning, Dad was asleep on the couch, so I knew things were okay. If Mom was really pissed, she'd have kicked him out.

"Like, what do you mean?"

"You're not a kid anymore," he says, leaning across the table. "I got plans. Made some good contacts inside. A few people owe me favours. I want you with me on this, little bro. I need someone I can trust."

The two guys who picked us up, Wheels and Jonny, come back to the table with trays of food. Henry opens the paper wrapper and stuffs half a burger into his mouth. His eyes roll to the back of his head like it's the best thing he's ever eaten. "God, I missed this shit!" We all laugh. He wasn't like this before. Jokey. I remember his heavy footsteps and silent looks. Like everything in the world pissed him off.

"How old are you?" Wheels asks. Again.

I look at Henry. He rips off another bite of burger and nods for me to tell them. "Fifteen." Henry and Wheels share a smile over a secret joke. But not Jonny. As scrawny as me, he's got a face like a skeleton with jutting cheekbones. He screws up his mouth and glares.

Henry tosses a burger my way. "Eat," he says. A bit of half-chewed bun lands on the table.

Another guy, they call him Rat, joins us. I get squished in the middle. He has a red bandana tied under his hat. I've seen him before. He works at the garage on Mountain Avenue as a mechanic. His hands are stained with oil, dark lines rim his fingernails, and he stinks like grease and gasoline.

"You made it," he says, raising an eyebrow at my brother. He has a scruffy goatee, buckteeth, and those kind of lips that always look red and shiny. "Who's the kid?'

Henry takes a long sip of his drink. I snicker at the long, low burp he lets out. "Lincoln. My brother."

"What happened to your face?" Rat asks me. It isn't like no one has ever asked before, but most of the time, I forget about the scar. Running from my temple to my chin, it covers a whole cheek. Mom always says I was lucky the water didn't hit my eye, or I'd be blind. I think I'd be lucky if the pot of water never hit me at all.

Now that Rat's noticed, I feel self-conscious and wish I could duck further under my hat.

"What does it matter?" Henry interrupts. He waits a beat for Rat to say something. The other two guys stiffen in the booth.

Rat just sniffs and clears his throat. "We gonna go outside and talk business?"

"Can I finish my fuckin' burger?" Henry asks. It's not a real question because his eyes have gone hard again. Rat shuts up.

I tap my foot, my leg bouncing under the table.

"You gotta take a piss, or what?" Jonny asks. He makes a face at the other guys when Henry's not looking. He doesn't want me here. I can feel it.

My cheeks burn and I hold my leg still. "You sure he's cool?" Wheels asks. His voice is sandpaper on my ears.

Henry presses his lips tight. "Ask him yourself."

Wheels looks at me like I'm a joke. "Are you?"

I nod. "Your mama thinks so." It's a lame joke, but their shoulders shake with laughter anyway.

Henry swallows his bite and takes a loud sip of his drink. He looks at each guy at the table and their faces get serious, ready to hear what he has to say. "You guys are my brothers. You're loyal. You could have ditched out, found another crew to run with when I went inside, but you didn't. You stuck it out, waiting for me. I'm back now. It's time for the Red Bloodz to make our mark. I got plans." My brother pauses.

We all lean toward him, listening hard. "We gotta get the chop shop running again." All three of them nod, so I do, too.

"And for that, we need cars."

Rat gives me an oily grin.

"And new recruits." Henry looks at me, his eyes steely. I start blinking and can't stop.

"Who are you hanging with?" he asks. "Besides the Polish kid?"

No one, I think. It's always been just us since the first day of kindergarten. He's not the friend people expect me to have, but that's their problem, not mine. "What's wrong with Jakub?"

"He's Polish," Henry says and wipes the inside of the ketchup container with his french fry. "You know, I never met a single Polish guy in jail. Not one. You know why?"

I shrug.

"Too busy working."

I keep quiet. I'll tell him another time about Koob's dad. How he looks out for me. How he let me stay with them when the pipes froze last winter. No water and four of us in the house. It stunk so bad my eyes still water when I think about it.

"We need guys like us. Wagon burners!" He says it loud to piss off the people around us. They look, like he wants them too. Henry raises his eyebrows at me and grins.

"I'll put the word out," I say, but it's a lie. I don't have other friends.

"Told you," he says to the other guys. "He's gonna work out."

My stomach is heavy with fast food. I'm squished in the middle again, now in the back seat of Wheels's car, breathing in Jonny's and Rat's fat, salty burps. Wheels drives down a street that looks like any other in the West End. Houses all built close together, their stucco cracking and roofs sagging. Lots of "Beware of Dog" signs and a few boarded-up windows. There's lawn chairs on front porches, maybe a case of empties. Barefoot kids with sticky faces run up and down the sidewalk.

The house we go to has people hanging out on the front porch. When the car stops and we get out, a *whoop* goes up. Henry gets hugs and back slaps from the guys. A few girls are hanging out in skimpy tank tops. One girl comes up and gives Henry a kiss. "Missed you, baby," she says.

"Welcome home," a guy says to Henry.

"Butch!" Henry yells. He's almost as big as my brother, with a long ponytail and the same Red Bloodz dagger tattoo on his neck. He holds his arms out. Everyone goes quiet when the two of them hug.

The guy gives me a chin nod. "Who's that?" Most of his teeth are missing. He runs his tongue over the ones he has, like he's counting what's left.

"Lincoln. My brother," Henry tells him. The way he says it stops any more questions.

"Come on. We can talk inside." Rat, Wheels, and Jonny go with them, on some silent signal.

I'm left on the porch. I don't even have pockets to stash my hands, so I stand there, cracking my knuckles because I don't know what else to do.

"It'll give you arthritis," some girl says. I didn't notice her before. She's rocking in a chair with ripped-up red material. The arms are shredded and the foam inside is popping out.

I know it's not true, but I stop anyway. No one else is paying me any attention.

She slouches in the chair. Her shirt's rolled up, or maybe it's just short. Her middle shows, a diamond piercing twinkling in her belly button. Her skin is the colour of coffee with lots of cream in it, but still darker than mine.

"I'm Roxy," she says. One side of her hair is cut real short, and the other side is long and dyed purple. When she rocks, it falls over her face, hiding her eye.

"Link," I say.

"What happened to your face?"

I lean against a post holding up the porch roof. "Got burned when I was a kid," I tell her, my voice low and quiet.

She shows me her arm. A long stretch of twisting, raised skin stretches from her wrist to her elbow. "Tripped into a firepit when I was eight."

"Shit," I whisper. She holds up her arm like it's something to be proud of. *At least you can cover it up*, I think. But I also think maybe she's the kind of person who doesn't want to cover it up.

Henry pokes his head outside. A cigarette is dangling from his mouth. "You good?" he asks. His eyes move between me and Roxy. One corner of his mouth lifts in a smirk.

I nod.

"You want a beer?"

Beer sounds good. Everyone else has one in their hands. "You want one?" I ask Roxy. She doesn't say anything, but gets up and follows me inside.

The screen door slams behind us. Henry and the guy with the ponytail sit at the kitchen table. Wheels, Rat, and Jonny stand around them. They all look at me when we walk in.

I slouch against the counter, trying to disappear. Roxy pulls two beers out of a cooler and passes one to me. The can is cold. My fingers leave prints on the frosty metal.

She nods with her head for me to follow her. Henry grabs my arm and pulls me down so my ear is next to his lips. "You gonna tap that?" he asks. The other guys hear and laugh, and I know Roxy heard, too. My cheeks burn, even the already burnt one, and I shake my arm out of his grip.

"Screw off," I grunt, but that makes them laugh louder.

I have to follow Roxy, even with all of them watching us. We go down a hallway and into the living room. Red Bloodz tags cover the walls.

It hits me that I'm at the Red Bloodz clubhouse. I get jittery thinking about how I'm drinking their beer, how I'm kind of one of them right now. How Koob would lose it if he knew what I was doing. Roxy pats the spot beside her on the couch.

It's dark green leather, the couch. It makes a sound, like letting out a puff of breath, when I sit on it. Across the room, three small holes in the wall stare back at me. Roxy moves close so our thighs touch. She's got a fairy tattoo on her foot. It starts by her toes and goes up to her ankle, like the fairy is flying away.

She leans her head back and sighs. Her beer is between her knees and it makes goose bumps all over her skin. I stare at them, thinking it's kind of ugly how smooth skin can hide all those little pimples.

Her bangs fall away from her face. I can see close up, she isn't much older than me. Piercings run up her ear and one is in her nose and eyebrow.

"You from the city?" I ask.

She shakes her head. "Reserve at God's Narrows."

"How long you been here?"

"A few weeks."

The beer is starting to loosen me up. I sink further into the couch and stop thinking about her ugly goose flesh, or how much of our bodies are touching each other. I dent the can with my fingers, listening to the metal pop in and out. More people spill into the house from outside.

"There's a room upstairs, you wanna see it?"

I look at her, like *why?* but she gives me a look. Like I should *know* why. My gut starts to churn and I wonder if she's shitting me. But she's already standing up. The dip in the leather where her body was disappears in seconds, like she was never there. I take another swig of my beer, draining it.

She crooks her finger around mine and leads me up the stairs.

JAKUB

Lincoln gives a low whistle. "You did that *last night*?" He tilts his head, pushing up the flat brim of his baseball hat. His narrow slits of eyes with their heavy line of lashes scan the piece, drinking it in. The piece looks even better in the daylight.

"Yeah. Where the hell were you? I went by your place at midnight and the lights were out."

Lincoln pulls the brim of his hat back over his eyes. "Henry's back."

I give a noncommittal grunt. "Is he gonna hang around for a while?" I pull my hood up. It's the last few weeks of summer, still hot out, too hot for a hoodie, but I like being able to disappear under it.

All I can see is Link's mouth. "Got a new tattoo. It says 'Brothers to the End.' Right across his chest," Link brags.

What lies did Henry spin to make Lincoln think the tattoo was for him? Biting down hard, I want to tell Lincoln that after a year and a half in jail, Henry has a whole gang of brothers. But criticizing Henry never gets me far. Some weird hero-worship thing keeps Lincoln from admitting who his brother really is: a criminal.

We walk toward the park, kicking a can back and forth. A few kids on BMX bikes are doing tricks around the fountain.

I pull my black book out of my backpack. A gift from Father Dom last Christmas, the book's textured paper holds the lead of my pencil and makes my drawings come alive. Not an inch of space is squandered. "What do you think about this?" I show him designs for a big piece, something that will take up a whole wall.

Lincoln pushes his hat back to see it better. He raises an eyebrow, but other than that, his expression doesn't change. "Think you're a king now?" There are only a couple of graff writers in the city who are kings. I'm not there yet, but maybe someday.

"Thought we could work it together."

"Another neighbourhood beauti-fuck-ation project brought to you by Morf-Skar Productions!" He holds his knuckles up and I hit them with my own. "Bam!" we both whisper.

A crew of Red Bloodz rolls into the park with swagger and red bandanas, five of them fanning out. Henry's in the middle, head shaved, his arms bare in a white tank top. Bigger than I remember. He doesn't look like anyone I want to tangle with. I wince at the tattoo on his neck. That had to hurt. He catches Lincoln watching him and gives him a chin nod.

Henry's muscles and blistering white undershirt make him look like a Roman god, perched on the fountain. "He wants me to join them," Lincoln tells me, so quiet it's like he doesn't want me to hear.

I narrow my eyes. "Are you going to?" I ask.

Sticking his fingers through a rip in the bottom of his T-shirt, he doesn't look at me. "I dunno. He's my brother," he says with a shrug.

"Who's been gone for the last year and a half," I mutter. I stuff my sketchbook into my backpack. A page tears. Valuable, thick paper. I zip up my bag, a couple cans bang together.

"Where are you going?" he asks.

"It's Tuesday. I have to help at the church." I sling my pack over my shoulder. "Wanna come?"

Henry's eyes are on us. I can feel them. Link probably can, too.

He shakes his head. "Nah, I'll hang here."

"He's not here to stay, you know that, right?"

Lincoln looks at the ground and nods. "But he's here now."

I have to go. Father Dom will be waiting. I can't force my friend to come with me, no matter how much I want to.

The best time of day to go to church is late afternoon on a summer day. Outside, the sun is at its hottest, the pavement baking. And in our sweltering apartment, with its one small electric fan whirring in futility, odours emerge, clinging to the heat seeping out of furniture and carpet. There's nothing to do but sit and sweat in the stink.

But the church is always cool; none of the heat finds its way into the silent cocoon. Smelling like furniture polish and old wood, it's the most familiar place I know. No matter how many times we've moved, there's only been one church: St. Mary's Parish. Invitingly cool, the heavy wooden doors slip shut behind me.

A side door opens and Father Dominic walks up the aisle. The white smock hides his ever-expanding waistline, compliments of the pierogi and braided sweetbread left on his doorstep by the women of the church.

As often as not, he shares his food with us. After all these years, he and Dad are like brothers, the only family either one has in Canada, besides me.

Father Dom walks with purpose, taking in the paintings, the stained glass, making sure all is in order. He pauses at the end of a pew, lays his hand on a woman's shoulder, and bends down to whisper something in her ear. With a sympathetic look, he stands and surveys the few of us in his presence.

Straightening some choir books, he makes his way to me. "Jakub." He says my name like Dad, the old way, making the J into a Y and accenting the *oob* on the end. Link says it that way, too, or just calls me Koob. Other people, like teachers, get tripped up on the letters and settle with Jay-cub. I don't correct them anymore. It's a losing battle.

"You're late."

I bow my head apologetically. Father Dom clucks at me. "You missed your father. He left a few minutes ago."

"Was he serving?"

"Lunch today. Bean soup. That old woman with no teeth asked him to marry her again."

I smile, feel my crooked teeth rub against my top lip. Dad could have been in the line for free lunch; instead, he volunteers to dish it out. "We help the less fortunate," he always tells me. "Dad, we *are* the less fortunate," I remind him. But he waves a hand at me like I'm talking crazy.

"You look like shit." A typical comment from Father Dominic. Beloved by all, with a mouth like a sailor. Raised in Yonkers, New York, by Polish immigrants, he's never lost his accent, or changed who he is.

"Late night?"

I twist around in my seat, checking to see if we're alone. "Did you see it? Up on the building between Strathcona and Mountain? You know, with the neon sign in the front window."

"I'll walk by tomorrow."

I stopped confessing my graffiti to Father Dom. He knows I'm not sorry. I'm sorry for sneaking out on Dad and lying, and for stealing cans of spray paint, and for the stupid tags I used to leave on people's garages.

The only time I've seen Father Dominic get mad, like spitting-when-he-talked angry, was the day I confessed that I'd tagged a garage the night before. Turned out, the garage belonged to one of the congregation. The old guy had come to Father Dom in tears about the vandalism on his freshly painted garage door. I promised him I was done tagging people's property. And I meant it.

I don't want to be just another tagger, laying scribbles down anywhere, like a dog pissing. I want to take what I do with cans of spray paint to a different level. But I don't have anyone to guide me. I'm self-taught. Other than Lincoln, I don't know any graff writers, at least not by face. I know the handles of the guys with serious talent, kings who are all-city and put up pieces that run for weeks, even months, in heaven spots; the best, most noticed spots that can't be cleaned away. But graff writers move like shadows, disappearing when daylight hits.

We settle into silence until Father Dom clears his throat. "Big match tonight. Wisla Krakow is playing Cracovia."

Father Dom has been trying to lure me into loving his soccer team, Wisla Krakow, since I was a little boy. He bribed me with their red soccer jersey for Christmas one year. I wore it non-stop for a few months. He thought he'd converted me, but I just liked the colour, and that it wasn't second hand.

"Your dad might come over and watch. You could join us."

I give a noncommittal shrug.

"Something bothering you?" A group of ladies shuffle past us, nodding at Father Dom, who puts his hands together and bows to them.

I finger the frayed cuff on my hoodie. "Kinda." He waits for me to say more. I look around the church;

everyone is lost in the solitude of their prayers. "Lincoln's brother wants him to join the Red Bloodz." Sunlight shines through the stained-glass window above the altar. Suddenly, the room glows with colour.

He lets out a long sigh and sits back, resting his hands on his stomach. "I hope it's an easy decision for him."

I shrug, wishing the same.

"I've seen a lot of boys follow this path, Jakub." He draws his bushy eyebrows together and frowns. "They end up in prison, or dead."

He isn't telling me anything I don't already know.

LINCOLN

Henry sidles over to me when Koob leaves. "Where'd your friend go?" he asks.

I glance at him. The dagger tattoo stabs me in the face, it's so close. "Church."

Henry laughs. "You shitting me?"

I shake my head.

"Church," he mumbles, like it's the funniest thing he's ever heard. "Why're you friends with him, anyway?"

You'd know if you hadn't been in jail for a year and a half, I think.

Henry doesn't wait long to hear my answer. "You're gonna have to pick sides, you know. At some point. Guys like him and you don't stay tight."

Henry doesn't know shit. Me and Koob are like brothers, course we're gonna stay tight. Henry points to his crew by the fountain. "You see them? They get it. They know what it's like to grow up around here. To survive."

"Koob grew up here," I tell him.

Henry flicks the brim of my hat. "I know why you wear that hat. You're hiding. That's what it's like to be *us*. You think your white friend has to hide? " He gives a chin nod to the guys. "They get it, little brother. *We* get it. The Polish kid, he'll never get it. The system was made for him."

What system? I don't get a chance to ask because a low-rider blasting rap music stops beside the park. It's Rat. Hanging one elbow out the window, he lays on the horn. Henry laughs and gives him the finger. "C'mon, you can ride with me. Those guys are on their own." He nods his head at the guys by the fountain. I catch Jonny staring at me. His boney face twists with jealousy.

So I walk out of the park with him, like he's the king and I'm the prince. Rat raises an eyebrow when I get in the back seat, but doesn't say anything.

Henry slides his hand over the dash of the car and whistles. "You do good work, man," he tells Rat.

"Wait till you see the engine. V8, 220 horsepower." They talk about cars in a language I don't understand, so I tune them out. It's nice being in a car and not walking. The tinted windows keep it cool. I take my hat off and let the a/c swirl around my head. Feels good.

We turn the corner, and the piece Koob did last night jumps out at me. It's a sweet piece. I lean forward to point it out to Henry and then stop myself. He's got no love for Koob. Seeing his graff writer name splashed up on a building isn't going to impress him.

Henry twists around in his seat. "School starts today," he says.

I shake my head. "Next week."

"Not for you." Rat pulls into a small parking lot on Mountain Ave. "Al's Automotive Repair" is written in faded blue letters across the front of the building. There are a couple of beaters and some rusted-out car parts along the side of the building. "Wait here," Rat says and goes to open the building. Henry and I stand in the lot. The ground is covered in crushed rock. I kick at it with my toe and a cloud of dust rises up, making my shoes all chalky, hiding the drips of spray paint. There's spilled oil stains in a few spots. Big, dark splotches that look like dried blood.

Rat rolls the garage door up, sheet metal clinking on the rail. Inside, there's a car on the hoist. Half the engine is on the garage floor. Tools and shelves filled with chemicals line the walls, and a layer of grime coats the metal chairs that Rat scrapes across the floor to us.

"This is where the magic happens." Rat taps a smoke on the back of the package. He lets it dangle from his mouth as he cups his hand and holds the lighter up to it.

"What magic?" I ask.

Rat gives a crooked smile. A trail of smoke floats out between his lips. He looks to Henry.

"After a car gets lifted, we bring it back here to the chop shop. Rat switches out the plates."

Rat turns his head and horks up a wad of phlegm. He spits it on the ground, but when he grins at me, a string of saliva stretches from his yellow teeth to his scruffy chin. He wipes it away on his sleeve and I almost puke in my mouth.

"Come on. You're gonna practise." Rat takes a putty knife and a long rod off its hook on the wall and we walk back outside to a blue car with a rusted-out body and smashed-in tail lights.

"You look like you're gonna wuss out on me." Henry narrows his eyes.

I shrug like I'm totally cool with it. "I've never boosted a car before, that's all."

Henry shakes his head, disappointed. "By the time I was your age, I was stealing three or four a week."

"Till you got caught," I mutter, too low for him to hear.

Rat jimmies the putty knife between the door and car and then slips the rod in. In five seconds, he's pressed the unlock button and he's sitting in the driver's seat. "Hot wiring's a bit trickier. Everyone's getting these immobilizers now." He frowns. "Older cars you can do the old-fashioned way." I climb in the passenger side to watch. "You gotta break the steering lock to get at the switch. Once you do that, connect the wires and …" The engine sputters to life.

"You try." Rat and I get out and he locks the car. It takes me a few tries, but I get the car open. The hot wiring is trickier. My fingers don't know the shape of things and fumble around.

Finally, I get it running and Rat high-fives me.

"The easiest way is to just wait till someone leaves the car running. Happens all the time," he says, like he's some Jedi warrior of car thieves. "Bump and snag works, too."

I laugh at the name.

"You pull up behind someone and tap their car, just give it a little bump. When they get out to check the damage, the second guy hops in and takes off in the car."

Rat pulls some beers out of a fridge in the back. A question's been lodged in my throat. "But no one gets hurt, right? What if there's a kid or something in the back seat?"

Henry kind of snorts and shakes his head. "You're not some kind of hippie, are you? Hanging out with the Polish kid made you soft. You're not a faggot, are you?"

You were the one in jail, I want to say, but I've learned to keep my mouth shut around Henry.

I shake my head, careful not to get too uptight about it. If he knows I don't like it when he talks about Koob, he'll just do it more.

"Hey, Rat, are you gonna use all that spray paint?" I ask. Cans of it sit in rows on a workbench, some isn't even opened.

He shrugs. "You could take a few cans. Al won't miss it."

Koob will be pumped when I show up with some free cannons. "We done for the day?"

Henry nods. "We can meet up tomorrow, give you some more practice. Here," Henry says and pulls something out of his pocket. "Little present for good behaviour."

The train yards smell like grinding metal, rust, and oil. Like dirt and gravel and black gunk that gets stuck under your fingernails. I let my pack drop to the ground and unzip it. Koob leans over to take a look. He gives a low whistle as I line up the cans of Rusto. "Where'd you get all that? That's like $50 worth of paint!"

"Didn't even have to steal it or nothing. One of Henry's friends gave it to me." I don't say nothing else, not what I was doing with Henry or where we were. If he finds out Henry wants me to steal cars for him, he'll lose his shit.

The street lamp turns the ground orange. Insects buzz around the bulbs. Masses of them. A lot of the train cars have tags. It's like a train graveyard at night. Quiet. In the daytime, wheels grind on tracks and machines are so loud you have to yell to be heard.

This is where Mr. K hurt his leg. Koob told me he couldn't hear the guys shouting at him, warning him about the load that was about to come down. Too late, he tried to run, but not all of him made it. I think that's why Koob likes to paint the cars. A "screw you!" for hurting his dad.

I hold a small bag up, dangling it in front of Koob's face. "Look what else I got." Four joints, expertly rolled.

"I don't want to be high when I paint," Koob says, shaking his head.

I laugh. "That's cuz we never have anything to get high *on*! Except fumes."

"Henry gave those to you, too?"

I shrug, pissed that he ruined my surprise. If I got them from anyone else, he'd smoke one. It's just cuz they're from Henry that he's mad.

There's more I want to tell him. About Roxy and what it was like at the clubhouse. The stories I heard from the other Red Bloodz about almost getting stabbed or out-running the cops. Glory stories, Henry called them. But the way Koob's looking at me, I keep my mouth shut. He won't want to hear any of them. "He's looking out for me."

"Is that what you call it?" he mumbles.

"He's teaching me things."

Koob's head snaps up. "Like what?"

The secret burns in my throat. "Survival skills." I grin.

"Henry's a boy scout now?" he says with a smirk. "You learning how to start a fire by rubbing two sticks together?"

In the distance, there's traffic, cars fighting to get up the bridge. I snort at Koob and shake my head. "Useful stuff, like how to make money. He thinks I can bring home a grand a week if I work with him." Just saying it made my stomach flip. How different would my life be with money in my pocket?

Gravel crunches under his feet, as Koob moves closer. "Are you dealing?"

Henry told me not to say, but it's Koob. I have to tell him. I shake my head. "Cars, man. He's teaching me to lift them."

At first Koob laughs, like I'm joking, but when I don't smile back, he shakes his head. "Shit," he says under his breath.

"It's not like what you think. Henry told me, when a car gets stolen" — I drop my voice even though no one else is around — "people get their money back, from insurance or something. It's like a win-win. We get paid and they get paid."

"Are you shitting me right now?"

I shake my head, thinking I probably should have listened to Henry. Koob's looking at me like I'm an idiot. "If someone's stupid enough to leave keys in the car, they deserve it." Henry had said that, too.

"He's using you," Koob says.

I back away, staring at the ground. "No, he's not," I mumble.

Koob takes a breath. "You can't see it because he's your brother, but he is. I'm serious, man. Do not get involved with this shit."

I look at him, but I'm pissed. I go along with *his* plans, following him up to the tops of buildings, sneaking out in the middle of the night to train yards. That's all illegal, but I do it.

"Henry's looking out for me," I say again. I can hear Koob breathing beside me and I think he's going to walk away, too pissed to paint.

We don't fight, me and him, ever. Maybe he's jealous I got something else going on, that Henry wants me to hang with him. "Pretend I never said anything about Henry, okay? I shouldn't have told you."

"You're gonna get burned."

I shrug. I don't wanna fight with him, so I let it drop. Him and Henry are like the angel and the devil, one on each shoulder.

"There's a car down there we could end-to-end." Koob says. His voice is stiff. He puts all the cannons back into the bag and slings it over his shoulder. I stuff the joints into the pocket of my hoodie. "Practise the piece I showed you, before we throw it up."

We walk along the tracks, balancing on the metal rails. I keep slipping off, but Koob, even with the bag, stays steady.

Between the train cars, a big yellow moon glows. Like an eyeball, watching us.

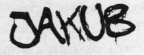

JAKUB

I crouch over my sketchbook, drawing. Sometimes, an idea pops into my head and I have to find a scrap of paper, a gum wrapper, anything, before I forget it. I see how people look at graffiti art that has meaning. They stop to take it in. They respect the artist. There are some guys with talent around the city right now. Creeping, like me, in the night and leaving behind a piece that forces people to stop and stare in the morning.

This new piece that's taking shape isn't about my name. It's about this place. A human head and torso, bound and gagged with a building for legs: half-man, half-structure. Looks good in my sketchbook, but throwing it up scares me. What if people think it's stupid and laugh at it? Or worse, a king tags it with TOYS, the ultimate insult to a graff writer. Tag Over Your Shit.

Dad comes home late that night, humming Polish folk songs. It's when I know he's happy, the quiet rumble in his throat making him nod his head.

"Jakub!" He claps his hands and rubs them together. "I have news," he sings. "Great news!"

He's been with Father Dom. They probably got into the Polish vodka people give Father Dom at baptisms and weddings. He has that loopy look on his face, his grin so big I can see gaps where he's missing teeth.

I don't smile back. I know what he's going to say. The letter arrived. Sure enough, he pulls it out of his pocket and wags it in front of me. "Accepted to St. Bartholomew's! As a bursary student. They'll pay your way, as long as you get good grades and stay out of trouble!" I lean closer to my sketchbook, hunching over the pencil lead as it scrapes over the paper. I don't want him to see my face. A private Catholic school in a good part of town, St. Bartholomew's Academy is the answer to Dad's prayers for me.

Dad grabs me and gives me a kiss on each cheek. His whiskers scratch my face. He lets out an explosive laugh of joy and punches the air with his fist. Shaking his head in disbelief, he mutters, "St. Bartholomew's," and raises his eyes to the ceiling and what's beyond, to heaven. To my mom.

He's excited enough for both of us. It takes Dad a minute to realize I'm not rejoicing with him. "Didn't you hear me?"

"I heard you."

He flaps his hands at his sides, like a flightless bird, and shakes his head at me. "What, then? This is a gift."

"More like a punishment."

Dad swears in Polish. "This place has done this to you! We're stuck in shit and you think it's where you belong."

Pushing away my sketchbook, I stand up. The West End is all I know. How would I fit in with a bunch of rich kids? "I get good grades, what does it matter where I go?"

St. Bart's was Father Dom's idea. He and Dad dragged me to the interview. I wore a collared shirt dug out of the donations box in the church. It stunk like mothballs. When we were at the interview, I looked at photos of the graduates. Rich kids from that part of town. I'd never fit in with them. They'd smell the poor on me. Schools like that aren't made for kids like me, no matter how smart I am. No matter how much I deserve the chance.

Dad frowns, desolation pulling at his face as he slumps into his chair. "That's what I thought about Poland. Your mother was the one who wanted to come here. I would have stayed, made the best of it." He's getting nostalgic; booze does that to him, too. I sit back down. He doesn't talk about my mom much.

"She wanted to come for our children, to give them a chance at a better life. She was brave." Colour flushes his face. "You think this is the life she wanted for you?" He stares at his leg, splayed off to the side, a useless appendage, like a stray dog that won't leave him alone.

Things would have been different if he hadn't gotten hurt at work. We'd be in a better place, not living month to month off his disability cheque or the kindness of the church. I know Dad stays in Canada for me.

He could have gone back years ago to be with his family. They write him letters, telling him it's better now, but he promised my mom we'd stay, no matter what.

He leans forward and grabs my wrist, his grip surprisingly strong. I don't try to shake him off. I look him in the face. His eyes, blue and bulging, are wet. "I want better than this for you. You get a good education, you can go to university, get a job. A *good* job. You can have a good life, Jakub."

A burner takes shape in my head as he talks. The images colliding in my head. A father and son, locked together, the eerie outline of someone angelic overhead. Father, Son, and Holy Ghost. A shiver runs through me at the thought of how it will look high above the street, in a heaven spot, for everyone to see.

"I heard from St. Bart's," I say. Lincoln and I are sitting on the front steps of the rooming house. They were painted green once, but footsteps wore the colour off, so now a strip down the middle is bare concrete. Laureen planted some flowers in pots, but after the dry heat of the summer, they've turned spindly and brown. Matching the rest of the place. Paint peels off in splinters from the window frames, and all five of the mismatched mailboxes hang at different angles, like cartoon road signs.

He turns to me, frowning.

"I got in."

"Shit," he groans. "You're going?"

I sigh. I don't have a choice.

Lincoln makes a face. "You'll look like a faggot, wearing the jacket and tie and shit."

I give him a punch to the arm, hard enough that he has to rub the spot I hit.

Our neighbour from the third floor, Lester, opens the screen door, lights the cigarette already in his mouth, waves the match to kill the flame and flicks it into the flowerpot. He nods to us. "You boys behavin'?" he asks in his lazy drawl. Spindly like the flowers, he's been living here longer than me and Dad. The day we moved in, he came down to help. There wasn't much to carry; a couple of boxes of clothes and some kitchen stuff, but Dad was useless with his leg. Lester and I hauled everything up the stairs. That night, Dad invited him for dinner as a thank you. He told Dad later he'd never been asked to anyone's for dinner before.

"Heard your news," he says to me, blowing a stream of smoke out the side of his mouth. "It's good, making your dad proud like that."

I roll my eyes. "He probably took an ad out in the paper telling the world. It's like no one ever got into that school before."

Lester gives me a long look, one side of his mouth tilted up. "No one who lives in a rooming house, that's for damn sure."

Lincoln stays quiet beside me, hiding under his hat.

"Any of those rich pricks give you trouble, you let me and Lincoln know. We'll straighten 'em out, eh?" He taps Link's shoe with his workboot.

"You?" Link glances up at him. "You couldn't take my ninety-year-old grandma," Link says, dodging a swipe from Lester.

"Later, boys," Lester calls and saunters down the sidewalk, the frayed cuff of his jeans dragging behind.

"Think he's screwing Laureen?" Lincoln whispers when he's out of earshot. "Saw 'em talking one night," he says, leering. "You know, like maybe there was more going on. She's not so bad looking."

I throw him a disgusted look.

"For an old lady," he adds. "Just wondered," he laughs as I pretend to barf.

A group of little girls walk past with Slurpees. Their mom trails behind with a kid in a stroller, screaming and arching his back to be let out.

"You think about what we talked about last night?" I ask. "About Henry?"

Lincoln pulls his legs toward him. "Yeah, kind of."

"You don't have to do what he wants just cuz he's your brother."

He shakes his head at me. "You don't get it, Koob." He sighs.

"Get what?"

"Me and you are different. I'm never gonna have a shot at things you will."

"That's bullshit," I fire back. "Did Henry tell you that?"

"He didn't have to. Now that you're in that school, you think you're coming back here? Working at the 7-Eleven? Or a factory?"

A girl we go to school with waddles past. Pregnant, her belly sticks out from under her T-shirt. A plastic grocery bag swings at her side.

I look at Lincoln, at how the taut, shiny skin of his scar is lighter than the rest of his face. "It's just a school. It doesn't change who I am. We'll still paint together."

Lincoln nods, but the corners of his mouth turn into a frown.

Dad puts a bowl of hot buttered noodles in the middle of the table. Father Dom sits across from me at the dinner table. "Father O'Shea, the principal, is giving you a clothing allowance to use at the campus uniform store," he tells me.

"Thanks." I nod, but keep my head down, shovelling food into my mouth.

"You see?" Dad looks at Father Dom, but points at me with his fork. "No gratitude! Nothing. He has a gift from God and he acts like it's a punishment."

"I said thanks, Dad!"

He blows a puff of air at me. "That was no thank you. After all Dominic has done for you!"

I put my spoon down. "Thank you for doing all this," I say, looking him in the eye. I turn to Dad, but he scowls at me.

It isn't the first time Father Dom has been pulled in as the mediator between us. He leans back in his chair and laces his fingers together over his stomach. "Opportunities like this don't come along every day. There's a reason it's come to you."

"Oh, yeah? You think God is looking out for me?"

Dad opens his mouth to say something, but Father Dom quiets him with a look.

"Yes, I do."

The matter-of-factness of his words shuts me up. It is what he truly believes, and I'm not going to argue. But if God is looking out for me, why'd he let my mom die? And my dad get hurt? I'd asked Father Dom these questions before. He'd given me his version of why, but what I really wanted to hear was that God screwed up, not that life isn't without pain, or that we all have burdens and God gives us as much as we can handle.

If that's the case, I'd also like to know, from God, exactly how much He thinks a crippled single-father can handle.

"God is not cruel. I know, sometimes, it might seem that way. I struggle to see his ways, too." Father Dom wrinkles his eyebrows. "But hard times push us in two directions. Either we accept them and look to God for help, or we turn away and let the devil take us on his path."

"You're getting kind of heavy."

Father Dom waves a hand at me and smirks. "Occupational hazard. Don't be a smartass."

"I told Lincoln about St. Bart's," I mutter.

"What did he say?" Father Dom asks.

I shrug. "Not much he could say. He doesn't want me to go." I look at Dad. "It'll probably push him closer to his brother. He just got out of prison, you know. He's in a gang."

I thought telling Dad about Henry would sway him, but my plan backfired. "More reason for you to get away from this neighbourhood," he says with satisfaction.

Father Dom nods in agreement. Arguing against them is a waste of time. I'm going to St. Bart's whether I like it or not.

LINCOLN

I can't keep my feet still. One leg keeps jittering on the pavement. I stand up a couple of times to pace the sidewalk. We're waiting in a bus shelter in front of a gas station. Been waiting for over an hour.

"Nervous?" Henry asks. He's got sunglasses and a baseball hat on so I can't see his eyes. But I bet they're half-closed and lazy, like we're not about to do what we're about to do.

"Just do like we practised," Henry says. Easy for him to say. He's jacked about a hundred cars. Gas fumes, exhaust, sometimes the smell of burnt coffee from inside the gas station store, are giving me a headache.

"Hey." He slaps my leg to make me pay attention. "That one," he says, pointing. "The Accord. He left his keys."

The guy went in to pay, maybe buy some smokes. Henry and I dart quick across the gas station lot and slide into the car. All of a sudden, my mind goes blank.

I forget what I'm supposed to do. *Shit!* I scream in my head. Henry's watching. I can't screw this up.

I look at the cashier inside. I can't see the guy; there's a pile of firewood in front of the window. "What the hell are you waiting for? Put it in drive!"

My heart's pounding. I look down. The gearshift. My foot's on the brake. I move it to drive, then press the gas.

We lurch a few feet ahead and then I slam on the brakes. I've only practised driving in an empty parking lot with Rat. On the street, there's too much to look at. Cars, people, signs; everything comes at me and I feel dizzy.

"Go!" Henry hisses. I press on the gas again, gently. Henry's slouching down in the passenger seat, keeping an eye out. *Focus,* I think. I turn the wheel to get onto the road, out of the parking lot, but I'm going too fast. I step on the brake again by accident and we jerk to a stop.

Henry slams his hands on the dash. "What the fuck, Link! Drive!" I kind of want to cry, I'm so scared and it doesn't help that Henry is beside me, breathing down my neck. I press on the gas again, careful to keep the wheel straight, but there's a parked car in front of me. Swear words hammer in my head. I know I have to switch lanes, but my mind and my body aren't working together fast enough. My foot hasn't come off the gas yet, and the car's coming up fast.

"Shit!" Henry yells. "Get in the other lane!"

Squeezing my eyes shut, I swerve. A horn blares and I speed up, flooring it to an intersection. I turn right, too fast. The car fishtails, but I hold the wheel tight until it fixes itself.

We're on a quiet street now and I loosen my grip on the wheel. Henry cuffs the back of my head. "I thought you were going to get us killed." I ease the car to a stop at the stop sign, no jerk or nothing.

The alley that leads to the chop shop is at the end of the block. I'll turn in, park in the back garage. The plates will be changed, and an hour from now, it'll be lying in ten parts on a cement floor.

"You did good."

"Thanks," I say.

"Think you can do it on your own next time?"

I kind of choke on the idea of a next time. "Uh, yeah, I guess."

Henry's eyes drill into me. "There's always a next time. And no matter what the club asks of you, you do it. That's what it means to be in the Red Bloodz."

I forget to brake as I pull into the garage driveway. In a flash, the chain-link fence is in front of the car and then I'm driving over it, mowing it down till Henry shifts the car into neutral. We stop inches from the wall of the garage.

"Holy shit," I gasp.

Henry leans back in his seat shaking his head. He gets out and slams his car door. My face burns with embarrassment. Rat's outside now, watching me reverse. He's waving his hands and cursing me out for wrecking the fence.

I reverse and park the car properly, but don't get out right away. I think about taking off on foot and running home. But they'll tease me even worse. Finally, I ease myself out of the car, taking a deep breath before I go inside the garage.

Henry pulls me into a headlock and my hat falls off. He rubs my head and slaps my cheek. "That's my boy!" His shouts echo off the concrete walls, the wrecked chain link fence forgotten.

Rat passes me a cold beer and clinks his can against mine. "Here's to a shitty driver and worse parker!"

I laugh and take a gulp of beer, wondering if anything will ever taste so good again.

JAKUB

I slide my arms into the sleeves of the jacket. The St. Bart's crest, embroidered with golden thread, shines on the chest pocket. Stiff and rough, like sandpaper, the collar cuts into my neck. But when I look at my reflection, I'm not Jakub who lives in a West End rooming house; I'm one of them, a boy from St. Bart's. The uniform hides the truth; that I'll have to wake up at 5:00 a.m., catch a bus, and transfer three times before I arrive at school.

"You need a tie." Father Dom holds up a navy one. "And a few shirts." We're in the Nearly New shop at the school, the faint tang of cast-offs fills the air.

"I have some here that would fit," the woman working at the desk calls to us.

The soles of the scuffed dress shoes feel heavy and stiff as I walk over. "Here," she says, handing me two shirts. "Try these." I wince at the thought of having the pressed and starched collars tight on my neck. And all the friggin' buttons.

"You don't like them?" she asks. She's got a tag clipped to her blouse that says "Volunteer."

"I have to wear one of these every day?"

Father Dom and the lady laugh. I hold my mouth tight. I didn't mean to be funny. The woman stops laughing quickly. "There are polo shirts on Fridays."

"What's a polo shirt?"

The woman walks past, and a cloud of perfume carries me along behind her. "These are polo shirts." Grey, collared shirts that feel like heavy T-shirts hang on a rack. "How many do you want?"

I cast an anxious glance at Father Dom. The principal of St. Bart's was willing to pay for a uniform, but I couldn't ask for anything more. Fumbling for words, I let my hands drop to my side and shrug at her.

She gives Father Dom a knowing look. "I'll speak to Father O'Shea, he'll understand," she says softly and grabs two of the shirts. My cheeks burn.

Father Dom stands with his hands in his pockets while the woman moves around the store, clacking through hangers until she finds pants that fit and grabs some thin, beige socks from a bucket. She doesn't say anything, but I guess my white sport socks aren't the right thing to wear. They're grey with dirt, anyway.

With all the pieces of the puzzle on my body, I stare in the mirror. It looks like me, but completely different.

"You look like you belong here," the blond woman says.

I catch Father Dom's eye in the mirror and he gives me a satisfied smile.

"Jakub, there's a call for you." Laureen stands in the doorway holding the cordless. We haven't had a phone for months; it kept getting disconnected. Laureen lets us take calls on hers. Not that there are very many. I take it from her and bring it to my ear slowly, waiting to say hello until I hear her shuffle halfway downstairs.

"Hello?"

"I'm on a cellphone! Henry got me one of the pay-as-you-go deals. In case he needs to get a hold of me."

I let a beat go by. Lincoln knows as well as me that there's only one reason a guy like Henry buys an untraceable pay-as-you-go phone. But I'm not in the mood to be an asshole. I drop my voice in case Laureen is listening. "What time do you want to meet up tonight?"

Link pauses. "I can't tonight."

My mouth twitches with disappointment. "I wanted to throw up that piece we did on the train. I found the spot for it."

"Sorry, man. I can't make it. I have to do this thing."

I don't ask him to clarify. He's choosing Henry over me. Rubbing a hand through my hair, I take a deep breath. It's temporary, I remind myself. In a day, a week, a month at the longest, Henry will get busted for something and Link won't have to choose between us. "Okay, whatever. Hey, what's your number?"

He hesitates. "I can't give it out."

I wish Link was beside me so I could slap him, wake him up from his delusional dream. "Pay as you go and can't give out the number. Got it. Sounds totally legit." I press the disconnect button and sit fuming on the stairs.

Laureen's watering plants on the front steps when I bring the phone to her. She's wearing an old T-shirt, so big her arms stick out like twigs. Her stringy brown hair hangs down her back. She smells like cigarette smoke. I look at the shrivelled-up sticks that used to be stems and wonder why she bothers. The water gets soaked up in a second.

"Father Dom picked you up today, eh?" Laureen doesn't leave the apartment much. She watches things from her window, keeping track of our life like it's a reality show. "Were you helping out at the church?"

I shake my head. "Something with Father Dom, but" — I use the line Dad has trained me to say if she gets too nosey — "it's kind of personal."

She raises her eyebrows and nods. "Everything's okay, though?"

"Yeah, we're good," I reassure her.

"I guess so, now that you got into St. Bart's!" She calls to me as I go back inside. I give her a wave and retreat.

My suit jacket hangs on the bathroom door. I pull it off the hanger and slip it over my T-shirt. I stare at the golden crest on the pocket. Once I get to St. Bart's, with the uniform on, and sit in a desk, I'll become one of the boys I saw in the photos. I get an ache in my gut, like a hunger pain, thinking about it.

Maybe all the shit with Lincoln and Henry is a sign. God's way of pushing me away from this place. I don't want to get messed up with a gang. I don't have a family connection, not like Lincoln. Dad's right; there has to be a reward for all the stuff we've been through. Maybe this is it.

LINCOLN

I'm kind of on a high after stealing the car. I wonder if anyone saw me, noticed it was me driving the car away. Taking someone's car is kind of anonymous, like graffiti. The thief could be anyone walking down the street. You just never know.

After I finish the beer, I wander out back. My new phone is in my pocket. I like the weight of it, how the screen lights up. I call the number I use for Koob. Laureen answers and by the time Koob gets to the phone, all the excitement about the car is bubbling up in me. I never had a rush like that before. I want to tell him everything, but Henry would lose it if he knew I blabbed. We don't talk long. Koob's pissed cuz I can't give him my number and hangs up. I'm not ready to go back inside the garage. I want to walk off the adrenaline, let some of it seep into the pavement like a trail behind me.

I head to Mountain and a girl is taping purple flyers up on poles. She wraps each one with packing tape, top and bottom, and moves on to the next one. Like she's planting a garden. She's done a whole row of them all the way down Mountain Avenue. I stop to look at one. "MISSING: Rachelle Fontaine." There's a blurry black-and-white photograph of the girl. Below is some information: how tall she is, that she has long, black hair and a fairy tattoo on her foot. I get a jolt when I read that and look at the photo again. It's Roxy.

"Have you seen her?" The girl shoves a colour picture in my face. Roxy's smiling in this one.

I shake my head. "No."

"Will you take a poster? Put it up somewhere. Anywhere." This girl has black hair, too. A breeze blows some of it into her face.

"How long's she been missing?" I ask.

"Couple weeks." Her eyes are tired and I wonder if she's been looking for her the whole time.

"Is she your sister or something?"

She nods. The corners of her mouth and eyes turn down at the same time, like her face is melting on the sides. "If you see her, call 911, okay?"

I walk away, past the row of Roxys, whose real name is Rachelle. She never told me she ran away. I carefully fold the flyer and put it in my pocket.

JAKUB

Painting isn't the same without Lincoln. It's lonely on the roof. The piece I've been working on looks even better on bricks and mortar than it did on paper. I stand back to admire it, wishing that Link was with me. It's real art, as real as any of the other pieces all-city writers are doing. This piece will get me noticed.

It's after three in the morning when I walk up the rooming-house steps. Some music from apartment 1D floats under the door, and a rhythmic knocking against the wall. Mr. and Mrs. Domestic Abuse must have made up. My key scrapes in the lock, turning with a click.

"Where were you?" Dad asks in a hoarse whisper.

I jump back against the door, my backpack slipping out of my hands. It clatters to the floor, the half-empty cans knocking together. "Shit, Dad! You scared me," I say, catching my breath.

Dad stands up, walks toward me, and flicks on the kitchen light. He's tired. His eyes are narrowed and puffy from lack of sleep. "Where were you, Jakub?"

I squint against the fluorescent glare.

"Out." I pick up the backpack and stash it in the back of the closet.

"What were you doing?"

My hands, blackened, sticky, and sore, dig into the pocket of my hoodie. I don't say anything. There are new drips of colour on my shoes.

"What's this?" He fingers the bandana that hangs around my neck. I forgot to take it off. Standing so close, I can see the folds of his flesh sag together; a few whiskers he missed shaving hide in the crevices. He moves past me and takes the pack out of the closet. He hauls it onto the counter and slowly pulls out my black book, a bag of tips, and three cans of paint. He bangs each one on the table with a metallic clang. The labels are smudged with colour and drips from the nozzle. Proof of my guilt. I wait for Dad to say something.

"I needed to know. Where does my son go until three in the morning?" He looks at the cans. "Now I know. This" — he waves a disgusted hand at the cannons — "is done for you. No more." It's an order.

"Dad —" I start to explain that it isn't what he thinks; I'm not some gang tagger wrecking stuff, but he holds up his hand and shushes me.

"This school is right here." He holds his palm open in front of my face. "If you get caught, that's it," he hisses. "I know you think — what you're doing — is so important. I see you working in your book. I ignored it. Coming home so late, the backpack …" He glares at the cans on the counter. "I thought, he's a good boy. Let him have his fun. In Poland, we would do graffiti, too." He looks different, harsh. For a second, I forget he's my injured dad. "But now, it is done." He stares at me for a long minute until I look away.

I think of the piece on the building. Of all the pieces I have yet to do. They deserve to be up somewhere. Other writers need to see them. I earned the chance to be known. But I hadn't thought of what the school would do if I got caught. Kick me out, probably. And what that would do to Dad.

I stretch out my fingers. They ache, the muscles cramping. My eyes burn from the fumes and my brain feels foggy.

"Promise me, Jakub. No more."

"Okay." But as the words leave my tongue, they're hollow. He couldn't take painting away from me anymore than I could ask him to stop going to church. I have cannons hidden under the back steps of the boarding house, a few in the garage, and more at Lincoln's. He can take away the ones in the backpack, toss the tips, but he can't take away graff writing. It's a part of me; Morf is my other self. We can't survive without each other.

LINCOLN

"**J**ust tell him what we practised," Henry tells me. He leans in close and I can smell the tobacco on his breath. "There are cameras on the walls, so keep your head down."

He spits a wad of saliva onto the sidewalk. A dude in a suit dodges the bubbly mess and throws Henry an angry glare.

Then he gets a good look at my brother.

I snort at how quick the guy's expression changes before he hoofs it inside.

We are outside the downtown mall. Middle of the day, people stream in and out the doors: moms with kids in strollers, white-haired old ladies, dudes looking for a handout, people in suits walking fast and talking on cellphones.

It's not a big deal, I keep telling myself, but my feet can't stay still.

"What are you waiting for?" Henry asks. He takes a

drag on a smoke and exhales out the side of his mouth. "Get going."

Inside the mall, palm trees grow out of planters and stretch up to the glass roof. I tuck my hands into my pockets and walk to the food court.

It might be nerves, but the smell of fast food makes me want to puke. Henry told me what the guys look like. I scan the tables till I find them: two Asian guys. They each have a fountain drink in front of them, but no food.

A security guard is standing right beside their table. He has a round belly hanging over his belt and a walkie-talkie on his shoulder. He watches the crowd. A couple guys my age are laughing real loud and shouting at each other, and he's staring at them. I tuck myself against the wall. The Asian guys have their heads bent low over their phones. They won't wait, Henry told me. If I don't show up on time, they'll bail. My feet start tapping again. I can't talk to them with the guard watching.

I check my phone, and when I look up, the guard's moved away, telling a mom she can't change her kid's diaper on the table. I walk quickly to the guys and slide into a chair.

"Hey." I swallow hard. My heart beats fast. I'm like one of those TV infomercials, telling people about the product. It's up to the Asians to make the order. If they want to take a look at anything, they'll go to the chop shop. My job is just to list the parts. And not get caught. It's the "not get caught" part that's scary. The mall is crawling with undercover cops trying to bust drug deals and all the other shit that goes on here.

One nods, but keeps his eyes on his phone. His thumbs move real fast, flying over the the screen. The other one takes a loud sip of his drink and stares at me.

I start talking, telling them what we have. I'm worried I'll forget something. Henry said I couldn't write things down in case I got caught. I wish Koob was here. He's better at remembering stuff than I am.

"How much?" one of them asks me when I tell them we have a Mercedes dash.

I shrug. "You gotta ask my brother," I say, just like Henry told me. His face stays blank, and I get nervous he's gonna walk away. I hold my breath.

He takes another long sip of his drink and stares at me. I want to blink so bad, but I keep my gaze even. My eyeballs start twitching. Finally, he nods and stands up. The other guy follows. I take out my phone and text Henry: *on their way*. They know to go to the mall entrance. Someone else will lead them to the chop shop.

I slide down low in the plastic chair and breathe, relieved I didn't screw it up.

Across the food court, a girl with a flash of purple hair and a hoodie with angel wings on the back walks to the escalator. I think it's Roxy, but can't be sure. I've been watching for her at the clubhouse, hoping she'll come back. I stretch my neck to follow her as she rides to the second level. "Roxy," I want to shout, but she'll never hear me. And Henry said I wasn't supposed to attract attention. I get up and go to the escalator. Maybe I can catch her on the second floor. The poster her sister gave me is still in my pocket. Roxy should know she's missing.

There are too many people in front of me to weave through them, so I'm stuck waiting to get to the top. When I do, she's gone. Disappeared. Missing, again.

My phone rings. I fumble in my pocket for it. "Where are you?"

"Upstairs."

"Get back to the food court," Henry barks. "You got another customer. He's sitting by the frozen yoghurt place. White hat. Link? You hear me?" His voice echoes from far away.

I take one more look. But there's no angel-wing hoodie.

No girl with a fairy on her foot.

JAKUB

I lied to Dad when I told him I was done with graffiti. It doesn't work that way. Dad doesn't understand what it feels like to be up on the buildings with the night wrapping around me like a blanket. The noise and buzz of normal life clears when I hold a can of spray paint in my hands.

Part of me wishes I could stop. I don't want to disobey Dad and I don't want to risk getting kicked out of St. Bart's, but the thrill of throwing up a new piece, of seeing *Morf* splashed across a wall, makes it impossible not to.

And with the first day of school looming, the jacket hung up on its hanger in the closet, I need to do a piece. Pushing Dad's disapproval out of my head, I flip through the pages of my black book.

How many pieces have I done before? Hundreds, counting all the tags. Twenty, counting all the really good shit, the stuff I'm proud of. How many times have

I been caught? Zero. What are the chances that tonight, the last night, would be the one?

Link's waiting on the corner with a backpack and more cannons. I don't know what Dad did with the ones he took. Probably tossed them. Thinking about all that wasted Rusto makes me shake my head.

I left the apartment with only my black book. I couldn't risk Dad catching me with anything else. I made him a promise, which I intended to keep. On weekdays. Once school started.

We don't say anything when we meet on the corner. Just a nod of greeting and a secret smile. I don't know what he's been up to all day, and don't want to know. Link's bandana sticks out of his back pants pocket. His cap, as always, is pulled low and hides his eyes. The days are starting to get shorter. At ten o'clock, there is only a hint of dusk left in the sky. Lincoln's scar is hidden by the darkness, the blindness of the night smoothing out the mottled skin.

The streetlights bathe the sidewalk in milky light. A few kids are outside playing, running after a yappy little dog that darts away when they get close.

"We're here," I say. A row of dumpsters lines the alley. One is under a fire escape. We can hop up, climb to the top of the building, and then cross the roof to the heaven spot, visible from Main Street and the bridge that crosses the river. Another piece ran for a while but got buffed last year. No one had thrown a piece up here since then.

Link pushes his hat to the back of his head and cranes his neck to find the top of the building. "Looks a lot taller from down here."

"Don't be a pussy," I say to him. He hates the tall ones. He'd rather rip off a piece under the bridge or on an alley wall. But those don't get seen. It's spots like this one, looming above the city, that leave a mark and get a graff writer noticed.

The dumpsters stink like rotten fruit. Holding my breath, I grab the side and haul myself up. A cloud of fruit flies swarms me when I make it to the lid. Lincoln tosses the backpack up to me. The thin, metal rungs of the fire escape are rusted and flakes of paint come off on my hands. I feel the stairs vibrate as Link starts climbing behind me.

I take a deep breath when I get to the top of the building. From up here, the bottomless sky looks like it could swallow us up, engulf us in its darkness. Walking to the edge, I peer over. A couple of people are on the sidewalk below, but the sounds of the city, the cars and sirens, die away. From the top of the building, the rest of the world doesn't exist; it's just me and Lincoln, and we own the city.

An emergency light by the door coats the rooftop and the wall we're painting with an orangey haze, highlighting splotches of bird shit at our feet. Lincoln's shadow joins mine on the roof. He sits down and puts his forehead on his knees like he's dizzy.

"You okay, man?" I ask, unzipping the backpack and pulling out the cannons.

His head bobs, and a minute later, he stands up and moves further away from the edge.

Colour from the old piece has bled through the white paint used to cover it. I open my sketchbook to a new drawing. Once we start, we have to move fast. The point of picking such a visible spot is that everyone will see the work when it's done, but there's also a greater chance of getting caught. Without speaking, Lincoln and I move around, getting things ready. I'll do the outline in black and then we'll fill it in together.

I stretch my fingers, clench and unclench my fists, and pick up a can of paint. The second it starts to hiss, a spray of black hits the wall, solidifying into something. It coats the rough stucco, giving presence to something ignored before.

We stand back when it's done. My shoulder aches from holding the cans and my fingertip is numb. Lincoln pulls his bandana down from his nose. His cap is on backward and his eyes roam the work, taking it in. I like watching his expression; it's a mirror of what other people will look like tomorrow when they see it for the first time. Lincoln shakes his head like he can't believe we created this. A smile creeps onto his face.

A giant fist holding a can of spray paint smashes buildings flat. They explode into fireworks of colour. It looks good. Even in the dim glow of the security light, the colours are vivid and it takes up a big part of the building. Our tags, Morf and Skar, are scrawled in the corner.

"Ready?" I ask Lincoln. He's packing up our gear. I stuff my black book into the back of my pants. From the corner of my eye, I see a red and blue orb spinning. "Shit!" I grab Lincoln's sleeve and yank him back from the fire escape. We lie flat on the roof, gravel digging into our cheeks.

Blood rushes to my head. I've blown it. My chance at St. Bart's: over. I slap the roof, curling my fingers into fists in silent anguish. What the hell have I done?

"Come down, now, you little shit, before we come up and get you." The voice is amplified by the megaphone.

"They think there's just one," I whisper.

"What do we do?" Lincoln asks, his voice raspy.

I don't know. My mind goes blank. As long as I stay up here, nothing is screwed up. Yet. I'm still going to St. Bart's, my dad is still sleeping at home, and Link is safe beside me. But the second we stand up, it's all over.

"We know you're up there!" the voice bellows from below. "Better for you if you come down on your own."

"Koob?" Lincoln looks at me, waiting for a plan.

"I can't get busted —" I whisper, but before I can say anything else, Link is on his feet, his hands above his head.

"Link! What are you doing?"

"Good choice," says the cop voice.

As he steps over the ledge onto the fire escape, the cannons in the pack knocking together, he looks at me. I stare at him bug-eyed, but he just shrugs.

"I got nothing to lose," he mumbles, and disappears.

My heart beats hard in my chest. I hear him land on the dumpster and then jump to the ground. "Give me the backpack," one cop says, quieter now without the megaphone, but I can still hear him, his voice echoing against the brick of the alley. "You want to tell us what you're doing up there, with five cans of spray paint?"

Link doesn't say anything. The cop shakes the cans. The metal balls rock inside, clanking against the sides and echoing against the brick walls. "Not much left in here," he points out.

I have to listen while they berate him. Ask if he thinks defacing property is a joke. Tell him it's vandalism and a punishable offence. That he needs to clean up his act, or face the consequences. Lincoln's silence a reproachful roar.

"Come on, we'll take you home."

"No point," Lincoln says. "No one there cares."

The cop snorts. "Yeah, well, it's what we do."

I wait a long time after the car doors slam to peek over the ledge. The alley is dark and empty. Forcing my body to climb down the fire escape, I can't get down fast enough, scared the cops will come back. Tucked against my spine, my black book digs into my tailbone. Gratitude for what Link did makes my legs rubbery, but I walk home quickly, desperate to crawl into bed and disappear from the streets.

LINCOLN

Friggin' cops.

Anger spills out my feet. They tap against the floor. It pisses off the cop. He glares at me. The vinyl seat squeaks every time he moves. I don't friggin' care. What's he going to do? Arrest me for foot tapping?

"You high?" he asks. He has a pretty-boy face, like he picked being a cop because he knew he'd look good in the uniform. Big eyes, long nose, a face girls probably like.

I don't answer, just stare out the window till the car stops.

"This it?" The cop turns around. A naked light bulb shines over the front door of my house.

I nod, keep my lips pressed tight together. First time I ever got brought home by the cops. Mom'll be pissed. I hear her brag about me still being in school and not giving her any trouble.

BLOOD BROTHERS

Dustin's light is on upstairs. I get a choking feeling in my throat. I don't want my little brother to see me like this, dragged home by the cops. I know how it goes, seen it with Henry when I was a kid. The sound of them hammering on the door and Mom or Dad shuffling down the stairs, half asleep, the deep voices explaining what happened while Dustin listens, confused because he thinks I'm one of the good guys.

The pretty-boy cop opens the door for me. The air smells smoky, like someone had a backyard bonfire. Or maybe a dumpster is on fire. The cop holds my arm. His grip is strong, but I shirk out of it. "You're hurting me," I say real loud.

I don't think about running until Pretty-boy loosens his hold on my arm to slam the car door shut. It's like a starting pistol firing Go!

I twist away from him and take off. My feet slap against the concrete. I push my chest out, barrelling into the night. Are they behind me? I can't turn around to check; it'll slow me down. I hear one yell, their voices tug me back. The car starts, but I'm free. A one-way street. By the time they get in the car and turn it around, I'll be hiding down some back lane.

I run. So hard and so fast, I think my lungs will explode out of my chest.

A laugh bursts from my mouth as I round a corner. I'm almost home free.

Ducking into another alley, I lean against a brick building, catching my breath. A smile stretches across my face for a second. Then my throat tightens because

I realize they know where I live. They could be waiting for me to go back.

I kick at a can in the alley. It bounces and spins against the pavement. The metal is loud against the brick and cement, and I wish I hadn't kicked it.

I hear sounds of traffic from the street at the end of the alley. The cops might be looking for me, trolling up and down the streets. They probably knocked on the door, woke up Mom and Dad, and told them what happened. I made it worse by running. But cops have better things to do than search for a kid.

I can't hide in back alleys for the rest of my life, so I stuff my hat in my back pocket and poke my head out around the corner. Headlights blind me, but I stick to the sides of buildings, walking slow like I'm in no rush.

My head clears as I get farther away from my house. My feet move on their own, guiding me to the one place I know will take me in.

Henry's nostrils flare, like a bull in a cartoon. But it isn't funny. He's pissed at me. His lips curl into a sneer. "The address is on my parole file. The cops'll figure out we're brothers." He shakes his head, fuming. "Why did you tell them the truth if you were just gonna run away?"

I keep my head down, staring at my shoes. I want to tell him I've never been busted before. Wasn't thinking straight. I didn't know I was gonna run until all of a sudden I was. But I'm too scared by the look on his face to say anything.

Henry swipes at the air and stomps a boot on the floor. Other guys cleared out of the room when he started yelling at me.

"Sorry," I mumble.

"What happened, anyway?"

I start to fidget. My fingers slimy with nerves. I can't tell him what really happened or he'll want to beat the crap out of Koob. "Got caught tagging."

He stomps his foot again, swears, and sits down in a chair. After a while, he calms down. "At least they didn't process you. Your prints aren't on file or nothing." He picks at his teeth, thinking. "You need a place to crash." It isn't a question, but I nod anyway. "Take a room upstairs," he tells me and I breathe out a sigh of relief.

I get up off the couch and I'm going upstairs when he calls me over. He doesn't say anything, just stares at me till I look away. I think about that look all night. It keeps me awake. Cuz I don't ever want him to look at me like that again.

JAKUB

Dawn scissors across the sky, tearing through the night clouds. Dad hugged me as I left, his stubble scratching me on the cheek. My first day of school at St. Bart's. He hadn't questioned the dark rings under my eyes, or the frown that etched itself into my skin.

I barely slept. The red digits on the alarm clock flicked by, and it felt like I was awake to see every one of them. I waved off breakfast, too, claiming nerves to Dad. I couldn't tell him about Lincoln, how he saved my ass last night. Or that I spent the night tossing and turning, thinking about how close I came to being caught.

My hoodie smells, like fryer oil and pierogi. I cringe against it, wondering if anyone else at the bus stop notices. I wish I'd worn a T-shirt under my hoodie instead of the dress shirt. It's going to stink when I get to school. I'll smell like the West End Polish kid I am.

Father Dominic bought me some pens, a sketchbook for art class, and a binder. The fancy zippered kind with a cloth top and lots of pockets, filled with lined paper and dividers. The colourful plastic tabs remind me of the stained-glass window at the church. Everything is stuffed in my backpack, beside the folded-up blazer that would be unfurled at school.

I wait at the bus stop with two other people. All of us quiet and tired, staring into headlights, waiting for the bus. Another guy joins us. Younger, with a scruffy beard and pock-marked face. He collapses onto the bench with a sigh. I feel him eyeing me. I don't need trouble, not on my first day of school. Looking over my shoulder, I meet his gaze. Tucking some greasy hair behind his ear, he stands up, using a pole for support. "What're you lookin' at?" he slurs.

I don't answer. The bus is a block away. I can hear the labouring engine gaining speed. I take a step closer to the curb. The other people waiting look at me with worried glances. They don't want trouble first thing in the morning, either.

"Huh? Buddy? You got a problem?" Drunk Guy moves toward me. He's looking for a fight. I can punch him if I have to. Wiry limbs don't make for good boxers, but I have a long reach. If this asshole is going to push me, I'll fight back. I shake my head and exhale a tight breath. The bus is slowing down, closing in on our stop.

A woman gasps and shrinks away. Turning quick, I see a knife glinting in the guy's hand. A small switchblade. His hand trembles with effort to hold it steady. The bus is in front of the stop now, and the air brakes gush as the door opens. The woman and the man with a lunch kit bolt onto the bus. I can hear her fearful, high-pitched voice as she tells the driver the guy has a knife. What if he leaves without me? He doesn't want trouble on his bus. I lunge for the doors and trip, my hands slapping on the steps. The driver reaches down and hauls me in. The doors flatten shut, almost catching my feet as they close. Drunk Guy hammers on them, yelling and cursing at me.

My hand shakes as I drop a bus ticket into the slot. "You okay?" the driver asks. He's a meaty guy, with glasses and a moustache. A travel mug of coffee sits beside him. The bitter smell makes me nauseous.

I nod and catch the eye of the woman who talked to the driver. She looks frazzled, her eyes wide and mouth pinched tight. "Thanks," I mumble as I walk past her and find a seat. The few other people on the bus crane their heads to look outside. Drunk Guy is kicking at imaginary rocks and waving his hands in the air.

As the bus pulls away, I slouch in my seat, holding my backpack on my lap. Just another day in my neighbourhood.

Three bus transfers later and I'm standing in front of St. Bart's. It's still early. School doesn't start for another half-hour, but there are lots of people around. The air is heightened with first-day-of-school excitement. I can feel it. I smirk at the parents taking photos: the kids posing awkwardly in front of the doors and parents squinting at the screen to line up the shot.

Guys reunite with backslaps and one-armed hugs. I think of Lincoln. We are both on our own this year, first time since kindergarten. Would he even go? Guilt stabs at me, looking for a soft place to dig in. I have to stop thinking about him, at least until school is over. I'll go find him when I get back home, find out what happened after the cops took him away.

Pushing past a group of guys, I enter the school. My locker is at the far end of the building, in an alcove. I hang up my hoodie and put on my jacket. Pulling the sleeves down and straightening the collar, I settle into it. I slip my tie, still knotted, around my neck and pull it tight to my throat. There isn't a mirror anywhere, but I know I look like every other kid. No one will guess I had a knife pulled on me or that it took me an hour and a half to get to school. Or that my best friend had been hauled off by the cops last night for graffiti writing, while I cowered in the shadows.

An announcement comes on the PA: all students are to report to the chapel for a service. I shuffle in, take a seat, and look around. Filled with five hundred guys, it's like no church I've ever been in. But we all stand and sit as one robotized mass when Father O'Shea gets to the microphone. His service is about the school motto: Brotherhood above Everything. I curl my toes against the stiff leather of my dress shoes. I can only think about Lincoln. Brotherhood above Everything is right, only these guys aren't my brothers. My brother is in the West End, probably ditching school and playing video games on a TV with a cracked screen, on a couch that smells like cat piss. My brother is the one who took the fall for me last night.

I'll skate through my classes, put on a veneer of a good attitude, make Dad happy. But there's no way in hell I'd think of boys from St. Bart's as my brothers.

My name was spelled wrong on the attendance sheets. The teachers call out for Jacob, not Jakub. I think about going to the office to have it corrected. But St. Bart's is a school made for Jacobs, not Jakubs. Jacob is comfortable in a blazer and tie; he belongs at St. Bart's. Jakub is the Polish bursary kid who eats lunch on a meal plan in the cafeteria by himself.

When the art teacher, Mrs. Zielstra, a short, round blond lady, bustles into the classroom and gives us our list of assignments, my stomach drops. Art class at St. Bart's isn't the cakewalk it was at Wilson High. A sketch due each week, plus in-class work. A kid groans beside me. The teacher pushes her glasses into her mass of frizzy hair. "Your first assignment, due Friday, is a sketch of someone important to you," she says. "I won't mark this one. I want to see your skill level. Begin."

I stare at the blank paper. This new sketchbook is a stranger to me. Same black cover as my other one, but we have no history together. It could be anybody's.

"Jacob?" The teacher looks at the attendance sheet and calls my name. "You can begin." A nudge to stop staring at the paper. I scan the room: a sea of bent heads, the sound of pencils scratching across the page.

I want to draw Lincoln. After last night, I owe him something. I think of his face just before he disappeared down the fire escape; a lump of guilt rises in my throat.

Then, another memory flashes through my mind. From way back, it's Lincoln holding my dad's hand on the first day of school. My pencil flies across the page, outlining a rough sketch of where the figures stand and the background. Later, I'll add the details, fine lines, and shading that make the people real, not just two-dimensional.

I'm so engrossed in what I'm doing, I don't hear Mrs. Zielstra walk up behind me. The catch in her breath makes me jump. "Oh!" she says. "My goodness, you're a talent."

My face flushes because the guys around me crane their necks to see what I'm working on. A couple of them snort in surprise. Others make a low whistle, impressed.

Mrs. Zielstra lays a hand on my shoulder. "I'm looking forward to seeing the finished piece." I've never had anyone, other than Link, compliment my work before. It feels good. I catch sideways looks from the guys beside me as we sketch for the rest of class. I'm not invisible anymore, sneaking around back alleys in the dark. Morf isn't the artist this time; I am.

LINCOLN

When I wake up, I don't know where I am. The room's murky, sheets cover the window and the mattress stinks. It takes me a minute to figure it out. When I do, I groan and wish it had been a nightmare. Getting caught on the building, running from the cops, the look on Henry's face; it all comes rushing back to me. My tongue is thick with sleep and I stumble to the toilet to take a piss.

A couple guys look at me funny when I go down to the kitchen. "Seen my brother?" I ask. "Henry?"

They ignore me, except for one who shakes his head. I stand beside the counter for a minute, trying to decide what to do. No one says, "Sit down" or "So, you're Henry's brother." They don't want me there; I can feel it.

I slink out and let the door slam shut behind me. I've got my phone in my pocket, but I don't have anyone to call. I squint into the sunshine and start walking. Don't even realize I'm on Koob's street till I see his rooming house is in front of me. It's like my feet found their own way, without me even thinking about it.

I stand in front of the building for a minute, empty lots on either side, trying to decide where to go next. Guess I could go to school, but that idea makes a bad taste in my mouth. Without Koob, there's no point. I don't get school the way he does. I want to, but I can only sit still for a few minutes, till the ticking of the clock hammers on my brain so loud that it's all I can hear.

"Lincoln?" I turn and Mr. K's limping down the sidewalk toward me.

He'll ask why I'm not at school. I hunch under my hoodie and try to come up with an excuse before he gets to me. "Hey, Mr. K," I call.

He waves a hand at me and holds on to the fence. I walk beside him toward the front steps. Mr. K holds the railing and sits down, pulling his leg toward him with a quiet groan.

It takes him a minute to catch his breath and then he turns to me. "Why aren't you at school?" He pats the step next to him, an invitation to sit.

I do it, but pull my hat down low so he can't see my eyes. "Doesn't start till tomorrow," I lie.

He grunts and I breathe a sigh of relief. "Jakub started today," he says.

I don't say anything, but it feels like when a knife slips and slices into my finger. The cut is numb at first, but then a rush of blood fills the space where there used to be flesh and it starts throbbing. I took the fall for him last night and look where it got me. If I'd let the cops catch us both, he'd be in trouble, but at least we'd be together.

Mr. K fiddles with the key in his hand.

"Guess he had to leave early," I say, to fill up the space between us.

He nods. "Probably won't be back till dinner, either. It's a long day." Mr. K sounds far away when he talks and I stare at my feet. The week, month, and year stretch in front of me, all empty without Koob to hang out with.

"You're going?" Mr. K asks when I stand up.

I nod, stuffing my hands in my hoodie pocket. "Got to meet my brother."

A funny look crosses his face. "Jakub told me he was back." He doesn't sound happy about it.

There's nothing else to say, so I raise my hand. "See ya, Mr. K."

"Anything you want me to tell Jakub?" he calls after me.

I shake my head. "Nah. I'll catch him later."

I start walking again, fast when I leave Koob's, so it looks like I have some place to go. I get to the bridge that takes me out of the West End, but don't cross it. Below, the river swirls, its current real fast like when a tub drains. There's cars and trucks thumping across the bridge, the stink of the exhaust pushing me to the path down the river bank.

Koob likes being up high, on the roofs of buildings. It's quiet up there. No traffic noises or other voices. Just us. But I never liked being that far from the ground. I like walking along the scrubby riverbank, tucked under the bridge, the tall buildings rising in the distance.

The concrete footing of the bridge has layers of tags tangled up together. Mine are in there somewhere, covered up, suffocated by others.

I pick up a stick left behind when the river rose in the spring. It's thick, more like a branch. Water ripped off the bark, so now its insides are its outsides, bleached white by the sun. It's a muddy river. Brown and murky, can't see two inches below the surface.

I stab the stick into the ground. It's baked hard on top, but the stick goes in. Not too far down, it's wet, and the stick sticks. It's a stuck stick, I think, and wonder how long it'll stay like that till it tips over.

I sit down beside the stuck stick and watch the little hurricanes of water swirl past me. The river's in a rush to get somewhere. Why? Maybe it should slow down and hang out for a while. I look at the stick again, how it's not moving, just jammed in the gummy muck below the surface of the ground.

I'm like the stick. Stuck. Not going anywhere.

I can't stand looking at it anymore, so I rip it out of the ground and toss it as far as I can into the river. But instead of floating, it gets sucked into the current and disappears, like being flushed down a toilet bowl.

JAKUB

I shed the blazer for a hoodie as soon as I get on the second bus and cross the river that divides the city. Slouching low in my seat and pulling the hood up over my head, I slip back into Jakub Kaminsky from the West End. The well-manicured homes turn into offices and then factories before the bus pulls into my stop. I have at least three hours of homework to get through and my backpack feels like a bag of cement, it's so heavy with books. I can't help cursing Dad and Father Dom for their great idea. They weren't the ones who'd be hunched over textbooks all night.

But if I'm honest, St. Bart's wasn't as bad as I thought it would be. In some ways, I felt more like me. I didn't have to hide that I was a good student at St. Bart's. It was the opposite. I *had* to work hard, or I'd get kicked out. And no one was looking to pick fights, trying to pump themselves up by pummelling someone. The toughness I needed at Wilson High was wasted here. Guys were more interested in showing off their cars than bravado. Or maybe the cars were the bravado: a wealthy kid pissing match.

I'm sweating by the time I open the door to the apartment, my shoulder rubbed raw from the heavy backpack. "Dad?" I call. No answer. I thought he'd be home, eager to greet me and find out how my first day was. Dumping my backpack on the floor, I fall down onto the couch and lie staring at the watermarked ceiling. My brain buzzes with the day and my stomach growls.

I think about starting my homework, but I'm too hungry. I pull a pot from the cupboard, open a can of soup, and let it heat up. We're out of crackers. And would be for a while. Those are the kind of extras that only come from a visit to the food bank, and it's two more weeks till the next one in the church basement.

Maybe it's thinking about dates, or standing in the kitchen by my mom's photo, but all of a sudden, my stomach seizes. I know where Dad is. Killing the heat on the stove, I grab my keys and bolt from the apartment.

"Why didn't you say something this morning?" I ask. We stand together at Mom's gravesite, like we do every year on this day. His hand used to fit on the top of my head when he said a prayer for her. But now, I'm taller than him. It's my hand on his shoulder.

"It was your first day." He shrugs. There are fresh flowers on her grave, but to the side are the shrivelled remains of a bouquet, their soft petals now brown and disintegrating.

He reaches up and puts a hand on my shoulder. We are intertwined, our arms braided together. His eyes get watery. "She'd be so proud of you." His hand grips my shoulder, rocking me toward him. The flesh of his finger swells around his wedding ring.

I used to come here with him a lot when I was little. Now, I just make the yearly trek on her birthday. With no memory of the real person, I think of her *as* the gravestone. Cold, chiselled granite; unbending. He thinks I come here to be with her. But I don't. I come to be with him.

I wonder how often he drags himself down here without me. There's a bench not far away, under a sprawling tree. The thought of him sitting here for hours, talking to her while I'm at school or hanging out with Link makes my chest tight.

A trickle of water runs out of the showerhead. And then completely stops. I look up at it with disbelief. I went out last night, after we came back from the cemetery and Dad's snores filled the apartment. I wasn't in the mood for anything complicated, so I ducked into an alley. Seeing Morf go up in block letters, covering a mash-up of other tags, calmed me.

The fumes of the paint and stink of the garbage mingled together. They should have made me nauseous, but I barely noticed them.

I went to bed not caring what I smelled like or that I hadn't finished my homework. I could deal with it tomorrow, I thought, when was my brain wasn't so cloudy. And now it *is* tomorrow, and I have to deal with it. But first, I have to get some friggin' water.

"Dad?" I holler. He woke up with me and was frying eggs for my breakfast. "Is there water in the kitchen?"

"No," comes his thunderous reply.

Shit. I can't go to school like this, stinking like a West End alley. I jump out of the shower and throw on sweats and a T-shirt.

Dad lays a plate of eggs on the table. The yolks wobble with my footsteps. "I can't, Dad. I have to get to school. I can use the showers in the locker room." He stares at me, a spatula in one hand. "Seriously, the bus comes in two minutes!" They won't go to waste; I know that. He'll eat them with a heavy heart, his effort wasted on himself.

His mouth sets in a grim line under his moustache. "This apartment! It's a shithole. Who can live like this?"

I give him a sharp look. "Bye," I call to him as I tear out of the building.

I arrive at the corner just as the bus pulls up, secretly relieved to be escaping the West End.

The locker rooms at St. Bart's are meant for the sports teams and are nicer than any bathroom I've ever had. Tile floors, a huge bank of mirrors, and trough sinks. Even the urinals are sparkling white. I take a long, hot shower, letting the water beat down on my back till my skin is bright red. I feel good, cleaner than I ever have been.

This early, the halls are empty, and I take my time wandering back to my locker. Would anyone know if I did this every day?

The library is open. The librarian nods at me when I walk in, hesitant. Dumping my backpack on the desk, I sit down and let the hushed silence envelope me.

Unzipping my backpack sounds like a roar in the quiet. I pull out my textbooks, their corners still sharp and new, and sit down. The quiet is disconcerting. I'm used to feet thumping up the stairs, floorboards creaking above, or people yelling outside. Even the pipes in the apartment are noisy; water, when we have it, gushes through, with each toilet flush.

I crack the spine on a book. Crapload of work for the first day, but I get it done. I still have a few minutes before class starts. The thought of hanging out in the hallway trying to find somewhere to fit in makes my stomach churn. I pull my sketchbook to me and flip it open.

The sketch of Lincoln on the first day of kindergarten stares back at me. I wanted to check in on him last night, see what happened when the cops dropped him off. But I hadn't. To be honest, I was shit-scared to face him. He'd taken a bullet for me. I want to think I'd do the same for him if I had to, but would I?

I get so into the sketch of Lincoln and my dad that when the bell rings, I jump. Packing up my books, I fly down the hall.

LINCOLN

There's no cars in front of the clubhouse. The door creaks when I open it. It's unlocked, so I figure someone must be there.

"Henry!" I call. "You here?"

The toilet flushes and the door opens. "Hen —" I start, but see it's not him. It's Roxy.

"He went out."

"Where've you been?" I ask.

"Around," she says and squeezes between me and the wall, so our shoulders collide.

I pull the paper I've been carrying around out of my pocket. "You seen this?"

Her face freezes when she looks at it. The purple bangs hang over one eye. "Where'd you get it?"

"On Mountain Ave. A girl, said she was your sister, was hanging them up."

Roxy pulls her mouth tight in a straight line and

glares at me. "You talked to her?" She says it like I'm a traitor. "You gonna turn me in?" She narrows her eyes and tilts her head, full of attitude.

I shake no, but she keeps staring.

"She'll drag me back to Buttfuck Nowhere, and I'll run away again," she threatens, even though I said I wouldn't tell on her.

"I won't," I promise. I want to say more, like, at least she came looking for you. But I don't. None of my business. "When'd you become Roxy?"

She shrugs. "When I got to the city. Didn't want to be Rachelle anymore."

There's times when I don't want to be Lincoln. Be cool if it was that easy. Pick a new name and get a new life.

Roxy/Rachelle takes the poster from my hands, and real slow, she tears the flyer in half and lets the pieces fall to the ground. I wait till she's in the other room and then I pick the pieces up. Her sister's number's been ripped in half, but I find both pieces and put them in my pocket. The rest I crumple up into a ball and toss in the garbage.

A wet spot of spit stains the couch cushion. I pull my cheek away from it and take a deep breath, trying to remember the night before. It was just me and Roxy for a while, but then other people showed up. The clubhouse was steamy, so many of us jammed in. There was music, smoking, beer, a bottle of Jack Daniel's. I wince. Thinking about booze makes me want to puke. "I'll never drink again," I mumble.

Someone else sleeps on the leather couch across from me. Other than the guy's snores, the house is quiet, now. Wiping the wet off my cheek, I put my feet on the floor and hold my head in my hands. The room spins for a minute. I stand up and shuffle to the toilet to take a piss.

The outside glows through sheets covering the windows. I wonder how long I've been asleep. The house is hot and stuffy. It might be afternoon already. I collapse back on the couch. Footsteps upstairs make the ceiling creak, like it's going to crash down on me. A few minutes later, Henry comes down the stairs, shirtless and scratching his armpit. I never saw him come in last night, but I guess he did.

He sees me awake. "Some things we gotta talk about," he says and goes into the kitchen. I drag myself after him. I hear him making coffee, pulling the tin out of the cupboard and peeling off the plastic lid.

There's another tattoo across his back, covering the space between his shoulder blades. I never saw it before. "West End," it says, in big, chunky letters with the Red Bloodz symbol underneath it.

The kitchen's a mess. Plates, cups, empties spilling out of the sink and all over the counters. I'll be the one cleaning it up later, I think with a groan. Henry hears me behind him and turns around. "Sit down," he says and pulls a kitchen chair toward him. Across the table, in the darkness of the kitchen, I see the dark circles under my brother's eyes, the way his eyelids sink down. He rubs his forehead and I think he's had too many nights of partying since he got out.

He tucks both hands under his arms and looks at me, all serious. "You're not cut out for this," he says.

His words catch me off guard. I don't know what he's talking about. I did all the stuff he wanted me to, stealing cars, meeting with buyers. "Yeah, I am." I fire back quick.

He stares at me and I hold his gaze. Even though my eyeballs want to come loose and fly around the room, I don't blink.

"I'm telling you, you're not. You're soft. You're not like me."

"I could be," I say.

He shakes his head, thick lips frowning. "Guys like you are a liability. They crack. I can't have that in my crew."

I stare at him like he's joking. His face doesn't change and I know that he's not. "Where's this coming from?"

He takes a deep breath and his nostrils flare. "I've been watching you, looking to see if you have any initiative. I'm not seeing shit." He raises an eyebrow, a challenge.

I sit for a minute, frowning. I'm trying to make sense of what he's saying, but my brain's fogged up like a steamy mirror. "What d'you mean, initiative?"

"Do more than follow fucking directions!"

"I thought you wanted me here. You said it was gonna be me and you."

Henry cracks his neck. "I got other guys to think about. A reputation. You can't just hang around, Link. Being in the Red Bloodz is more than that. You gotta man up. Show the other guys you aren't a pussy." He stands up. "Make some coffee. I'm going to take a shower. You should, too. You look like shit."

Before he leaves the kitchen, he turns back to me. "You want in, you got to earn it, like everyone else." His heavy feet stomp upstairs. I think about leaving right then. Telling him to make his own frickin' coffee and racing out of the clubhouse.

But I got nowhere else to go.

I peel off the lid on the coffee can. I don't know how much coffee to put in, so I dump in half of it and pour in the water. In a few minutes, the slow drip of brown blood fills up the glass pot.

Part of me knows Henry's right. I'm not cut out for this life, not like him. He's giving me a way out. Maybe I should take it.

But without Koob or Henry, I'm not part of anything. A stray dog with no bite. At least with the Red Bloodz, I got a crew, guys who have my back.

Koob's got a new life, going to that school. Guess it's time for me to get one, too.

Roxy comes in, walking slow and holding a wall like she's going to fall down. "My head's killing me. You got any Tylenol?"

I shake my head.

"Any juice in the fridge?" She rubs a hand across her forehead.

"You can check."

She slumps down in a chair like she's eighty years old. "Can you? The room is spinning."

Fridge is empty, except for some mouldy cheese and cream that comes out in a clump. "You want coffee?"

"Okay."

There's more movement in the house, coughing, another toilet flushing, low voices. "How long you been here?" I ask and pass her a chipped coffee mug, filled halfway up.

"Off and on since I left the rez. A girl I knew was partying with them one night. I came along and kinda never left."

"No one gets on your case about it? You hanging around?"

Roxy flicks me a look from under her bangs. "Not till now."

"I'm not. I just wondered how it works if you're not one of them."

"A Red Bloodz, you mean?"

I nod.

"You thinking about joining?"

"Maybe. I been doing some work for them." Something to fill the empty spot Koob left.

Rat passes the kitchen on his way to the front door. His jacket is in his hands and one boot's not laced up. "Hey, Lincoln. You see Henry, tell him to come by the garage."

"He's having a shower," I say. "Hey, uh, Rat?" I take a few steps close to him so Roxy's behind me. "You got any more work, I'm good for it."

He gives me a slow nod. "Yeah, okay. Come by later. We got a meet tonight. Maybe you can handle it."

"Hell yeah," I say and want to fist-bump him, but don't. Instead, I put on my best gangland sneer and pull my hat down. I might not be the guy Henry wishes I was, but that didn't mean I couldn't become him. Like Mr. K's always saying, if I put my mind to something, who knows what I can do.

Rat arranged it so it was just me and him going to the meet. Without Henry, I wasn't nervous. Told the guys what we had to offer and let them work out the details with Rat. Easy-peasy. By the time I got back to the garage, Rat was turning lights off and calling it a day. "Here," he said, handing me some cash. "It's your cut."

I flipped through the money. "You shitting me?" Two hundred dollars!

"I'll keep it if you think it's too much," he says.

"No way, man!" I stuff it in my pocket and squeeze my fist around it, worried it'll fall out. We go separate ways when we leave the garage. Rat toward the clubhouse, but me, a different direction. I've never had this much money to spend how I want. I wish Koob was with me. Be more fun to go into stores with him, but I push that thought out of my head. I earned the money, guess it's mine to spend.

Mom and Dustin are sitting on the couch. She's got a bag of chips in one hand and a can of pop in the other. She takes one look at me when I walk in the door and shakes her head. "What's that?" she asks.

"What do you mean?" I play dumb, and hold the box up, waving it to Dustin. He looks up from his video game and his jaw drops.

"Where'd you get that?"

Dustin runs over and tears into the box. Cardboard goes flying as he peels it away from the plastic window.

"At a store."

"What's in the bag?" she says, eyeing it up. A new jacket, warm for winter, stuffed with feathers; it's so big it looks like I'm lugging a pillow around with me.

"Jacket. One of those parkas I've been wanting."

"Huh? Since when do you have money for all this?"

"Got a job," I tell her.

She narrows her eyes at me. "Doing what?"

"None of your business," I say, pissed that she's ruining the fun. That's Dad's complaint about Mom, too. She shuts the party down just when it's getting started.

She gets up from the couch, faster than I think she can move, and rips the box out of Dustin's hands. "My house, my business."

Dustin's eyes are big as he stares at his toy.

If I tell her I'm working with Henry, she'll lose it. "Koob's dad helped me. He knew someone looking."

"Doing what?" she asks again, and I'm trying to think fast. "At the church. I sweep up and stuff. Few hours a week, but it pays good."

She holds the car in her hands, like a hostage. My eyes are flitting around the room. "What?" I say. "You think I'm lying?"

Passing Dustin the toy, she shoots me a look. I fire it back at her. "I'm gonna call him and find out," she threatens, but I know she won't.

I go up to my room, lugging the bag with me. A few minutes later, I hear the whir of the car as Dustin gets the batteries in. Listening to him laugh makes me think playing the game, stealing the cars, might be worth it.

JAKUB

Dad left a note, like an invitation, telling me to join him at St. Mary's. It's a feast day, Birth of the Virgin Mary. I let the note drop back to the table. Dad and twenty old Polish ladies will huddle in pews, listening to Father Dom's voice echo off the marble floor.

I change into jeans and a T-shirt, carefully hanging my jacket in the front closet. Even secondhand, it is the nicest piece of clothing we own.

"Koob!" I hear my name shouted from outside. With the windows open, Link's voice carries up. "Koob!" he calls again.

I open the window wider and lean out. There he is, in the front yard, like nothing happened. "Be down in a minute." I finish changing, all the things I want to say to him running through my head.

He's checking his phone when I get outside, and wearing a new, brand-name jacket, too heavy for the weather. He must be sweating under it.

"Whoa!" I say, taking in the jacket.

Lincoln nods and grins. "Never had nothing this nice before."

"You win the lottery?" I ask.

He pulls some bills from his pocket. "Working," he says nonchalantly.

I take a few steps closer. "Shit! Where'd you get all that?" I look around, nervous he'll get jumped. "Put it away!"

He stuffs it back into his pocket, but the smile stays. "Told you Henry was looking out for me. That's from one week's work."

"Are you messing with me?"

"No, man. There's more where this came from, too. It's steady, long as I bring them what they want." Lincoln lowers his head and talks to me out of the side of his mouth. "I lifted two last night. Just walked down the street, checking door handles. Found two that weren't locked, and …" He shrugs, like I should know the rest.

"What if you get caught?" I ask.

"What can they do? Young offender," he says with a shrug. "Maybe get some community service."

"So, you just lift the car and that's it? Your work is done?"

"Drive it to the garage, and then, yeah, I'm done." A hint of a smile tugs at Link's mouth. "You interested?"

Staring at the ground, I kick at a weed in the sidewalk with my shoe and shake my head. He makes it sound easy, but there's always a catch.

Link moves in closer and lowers his voice. "I didn't think I was either, man. I was shit-scared the first time. But I'm getting good at it." He holds up his hands for me. "Quick fingers," he says and grins.

"I wouldn't brag about it."

Link shoots me a look. "*You* do. I hear about the pieces you throw up all the time. What's the difference?"

There's no comparison between graff writing and what he is doing. "I'm not stealing cars!"

"You're vandalizing, trespassing. Koob! I've been with you. I been *busted* for you. I know what we do. I know what happens when we get caught."

I shake my head. "I didn't tell you to go down the ladder. You went cuz you wanted to." I sound like an asshole. The apology I want to give him evaporates. He's got the upper hand, wearing his new jacket, with cash left in his pocket; I don't know how he's going to play it.

"I went with the cops to help you. I thought that's what we did, look out for each other."

I take a deep breath. A siren blares a couple blocks away. Seeing Link like this, puffed up in his jacket, makes me feel farther from him than when I'm at school.

We stand toe-to-toe, neither one backing down.

"I coulda let them take you, too," he says quietly.

I go back to kicking the weed with the toe of my shoe. As much as I want things to be normal between us, he's making it hard for me. The balance is shifted and I can't find my footing.

"So I owe you one?"

"More than one," he says, and I wonder how bad he got it from his mom when he showed up with cops on the doorstep. I've seen her ream out her kids pretty hard, not that it did any good in Henry's case.

The siren gets louder and a cruiser races down our street, a blur of lights and sound. Link follows it with his eyes. "I trust you, Koob. When we go up on buildings to do a piece, I always follow. How come you don't trust me like that?"

His words catch me off guard. I wish I could shrug them away, but they're too heavy for that.

I look at Link, my best friend. The only brother I've ever had. He's never asked me for anything before. When I wake up tomorrow, I'll leave the West End. For a few hours every day, I get to escape. He doesn't. He's stuck here on his own. "What do you want me to do?"

He pulls a piece of paper out of his pocket. "I just wanna know if you ever seen any of these cars at your school."

I scan the list and pass it back to him with a snort. "You're fucking crazy. I'm not helping you lift cars from my school!"

"You don't gotta help me! I just need to know if they're there. I do the rest. I'll even give you a cut of whatever we make."

I want to smack him, give him a wallop that sends him flying to the curb. *This* is his idea?

"Henry told me to show some initiative," he says quickly. "That's all I'm doing. If I could just lift one really good ride, it would show him I have what it takes."

"I'm not helping you," I say and turn to go back inside.

"What if I said I was going to do it anyway? Even if you don't help me?"

"Go ahead. Get busted." He's trying to bluff me, but it won't work.

"I already was, remember? You just apologized for it ten seconds ago when you said you owed me."

"And this is what I owe you?"

Link nods.

"Hanging out with your brother has messed you up."

Link's eyes narrow and he starts blinking. "You care so much about the guys at school?"

"No!" I throw my hands up. "I don't give a shit about them!"

"Then what's the big deal?"

He didn't get it. "You want me to steal cars." I say it slow, so he'll hear how crazy it sounds. "If we get caught, I get kicked out. Dad would never forgive me for doing something like this."

But he persists. "One time, Koob. That's all. Let me score a sweet ride and I swear, I'll never ask again."

"And that's it? You'll have proven to Henry you can do it and you'll be done?" I ask, incredulous.

Link nods his head. "Yeah. I swear. Come on. Me and you, together. How it's supposed to be." Link cajoles, holding up his fist for a bump. "Like old times, except different."

How many nights had we gone out, hidden in darkness, and worked side by side creating something amazing? Those days might never happen again if I say no to him. He's standing in front of me, fist in the air.

"Don't leave me hanging," he says.

Reluctantly, mine goes up too and they collide.

LINCOLN

'm pumped when I leave Koob's. It feels good to have him back.

This is just what Henry was talking about, showing some initiative, working an angle. I didn't think Koob was going to say yes, but I convinced him. Me. I never convinced nobody to do anything before.

I get to my house and the screen door slams, bouncing in the frame. It's flimsy and bent from so many openings and closings.

"Hey, Dusty," I say. The kid's sitting on the couch in zombie mode, watching TV. I come up from behind to put him in gentle chokehold. I get him down in a wrestling move, and he tries his hardest to get free. His body is wiry and thin, like I used to be, and I can see his muscles straining through his skin. Mom gave him a buzz cut for the summer. It's grown out a bit. I rub my cheek against his soft, little-kid hair.

Finally, I let go and he tries a roundhouse kick before flopping back onto the couch.

I listen for anyone else, but the house is quiet except for the TV. "Where's Mom?"

"Doing laundry." At the laundromat a block away. How many hours did I spend in that place watching other people's gitch spin around? Guess by the third kid, she's given up dragging him with her.

I open the fridge. The wire shelves are pretty much empty. There's a pack of baloney and a loaf of bread. "You want a sandwich?" I call to him.

"Yeah."

Slapping mustard, the meat, and bread together, I bring it out to him. "You go to school today?" I ask.

Dustin shakes his head. He chews his sandwich. The remote-control car I bought him is in the corner. A couple wires stick out of the bottom. "You break it already?" I ask.

He shrugs. "Wanted to see how it worked."

I snort and shake my head. Mad for a second, but then I think, I woulda done the same thing when I was a kid.

There's a grunt at the door and Mom walks in, a garbage bag full of laundry in her arms, like she's Santa. She looks at me. Her eyes wander to the half-eaten sandwich in my hands. "When'd you get here?" she asks and drops the bag of laundry on the floor.

"Little while ago."

She's breathing hard from the walk. "That baloney's for Dustin's lunch."

I let the sandwich drop to my plate. "You gonna take him tomorrow?" I ask. It was never her who made sure I got up in the morning; it was Koob and Mr. K. They'd bang on the door till I answered and wait for me on the front steps. We'd walk together, me and Koob running ahead and then waiting on corners for Mr. K to catch up.

"Watch your mouth," she says, hands on hips. Dustin puts down his sandwich like he's not sure if he's supposed to eat it or not.

I see her eyes wander to my jacket. "Been with your brother?"

"Is that why you're pissed? Cuz I'm hanging out with Henry?"

She gets real quiet, like the air before a storm hits. I kind of cringe in my jacket, waiting for what she's gonna say next. "One minute, the cops are banging on our door, and the next, you're showing up with toys for Dustin." She shakes her head. "And here you are. No explanation or nothing. Just sitting on the couch eating food that's not yours."

"You weren't home," I fire back. And then I'm mad. I jump off the couch, and the plate with my sandwich falls to the ground, the mustard splattering on the floor. She turns her back to me and carries the bag of laundry up the stairs. But she's big and the bag is awkward, and she looks like an elephant lumbering away. "Fat cow," I mutter after her.

"What'd you call me?" She drops the laundry, turns around, and glares.

"Nothing," I mumble.

She takes a step toward me and I take one back. She's scary when she's mad, and I want to get out of her way. "Get out. Go back to wherever the hell you've been." She says it quiet so I know she means it. She only yells when it's for show.

"Are you kicking me out?"

"I don't want cops coming around again. It's bad for Dustin."

It doesn't answer my question, but her eyes are squished up through her glasses. I look over at my little brother. He turns back to the TV, pretends like he hasn't been listening. Pushing the sandwich away, he lies down on the couch, probably wondering if I'm one of the good guys or not.

The screen door slams after me, echoing down the street. She's pissed I'm hanging with Henry, but she just kicked me out, so where does she think I'm gonna go?

I think about going to Koob's, asking if I can crash at his house till she calms down, but he'll go to school tomorrow. Mr. K won't want me hanging around all day.

My new jacket is hot and I'm sweating under it. The baloney left a slimy, spicy coating on my tongue and I wish I'd never eaten it.

I wasn't even hungry.

JAKUB

Honda Acord
Honda Sivik
Toyota Camry
Jeep Grand Chairoky
Toyota Karola
Nisan Ultima
Ford Explorer

I look at the list written in Lincoln's sloppy printing. It takes up one page in my art book.

"These are the ones we look for. But you know, if you see something good just sitting there, unlocked, or keys in the ignition, we'll jump on it, too." I thought about the car idling in the parking lot the other day, ripe for the picking.

He hands me a cellphone. "This one's yours. Text me with the plate and what kind of car. If anything goes sideways, ditch the phone."

I nod, but feel the colour drain from my face. I pass him a plastic bag bulging with a blazer lifted from the change room in the gym. He pulls it out and his lips curl in a smile. "This is all it takes to look like one of you, eh?"

I snort. "I'm not one of them." But even as I say it, I feel like a hypocrite. I like the feeling of walking into St. Bart's, wearing the blazer, knowing I belong there. I just can't tell Link that.

"You know what I mean." He rubs his thumb across the golden shield on the pocket, then slips his arms into the sleeves. With only a T-shirt on underneath, his neck looks scrawnier than usual poking out of the collar.

I get a sick swell in my stomach watching him. Link narrows his eyes at me. "You're not going to bail, right?"

I shake my head. Link thinks we could get a grand for each car he's able to lift, maybe more if it's a luxury model. I'm not doing this for the money, I remind myself, even though a $60,000 SUV would buy a whole lot of groceries.

But the doubt is starting to settle in, and my mouth goes dry. I look at the phone in my hand. All I have to do is send a text. I'm not the one lifting the car, or driving it out of the lot. But if we get caught, it'll mean police, expulsion, public humiliation. Stealing cars is a lot more serious than graffiti. Even if Henry thinks a J.D. won't get more than community service, Dad would be ashamed of me. Explanations about Lincoln needing my help would be pointless.

"My number's already programmed into the phone," Lincoln says. "Don't use it for anything else."

"I won't," I promise. I find the number, committing it to memory just in case. "You'll meet me at the bus stop at six tomorrow, right?"

Link nods. He'll cross over with me, wearing the school jacket, disguising who he really is. He slaps my back and I think I might throw up.

After school tomorrow, I'll go to confession. Father Dom will sit beside me shaking his head in disbelief. Then rant at my poor judgment. But he'll take my confession. He has to.

LINCOLN

stuff the jacket into the bag as I walk away from Koob's place. I wish I hadn't seen the look on his face; he looked shit-scared. Guess it's different when you got something to lose. All I've got is something to gain. If I show up at the chop shop with a high-end car and Rat sells off the parts, Henry's going to forget about me being a liability. *That's* the kind of shit that shows initiative.

I take the stairs to the clubhouse two at a time. Couple of the guys are playing vids, a few others eating pizza; one girl is stoned and sitting on someone's lap, staring at her hand. "Where's Henry?" I ask.

No one answers, so I go to the table where the guys are eating a pizza. I reach my hand to take a slice, but Jonny slaps it away, like I'm a dog nosing for scraps.

I shoot him a look, but he ignores me and keeps talking to his friends. "Where's my brother?" I say again. This time, they all look at me.

"Out back," Jonny says and burps in my face. He's

got a shiner. New, it's red and swollen. There's a cut across his nose, too, but I don't ask where he got it. There's lots that happens around here that stays quiet. Asking questions draws attention, and that's the last thing any of these guys want.

I open the back door off the kitchen. It's wooden and sticks a little, so the glass in the window rattles. Henry's talking with Butch, and they both turn to look at me, their eyes hard, and I know it was stupid to interrupt.

"What?" Henry barks.

I squeeze the doorknob and wish I could duck inside. "Nothing," I say.

Henry looks at me like I'm a child, half-shaking his head and frowning. "Then get the fuck out of here."

Jonny opens the fridge to get a beer, and I hear him snort at me. "You're a fucking child," he slurs, scowling. "You walk around like having Henry as your brother automatic — automatic —" He tries to wrap his lips around the word, and gives up. "Gets you a spot in the clubhouse." He takes a step closer to me and puts his beer on the counter. "You got to earn it, you little shit."

He's got a look in his eye, the one that's not swollen, like he wants to pound me. I ball my hands up into fists, tensing my arm. I'll have to fight back, make a show of it, even though Jonny's got a couple inches and fifty pounds on me. He's eyeing up my jacket and I wonder if that's what he's pissed about. That I'm getting a piece of the action?

I want to bolt, but Jonny's blocking the kitchen door. Henry and Butch are outside. I could run that way, but Henry would make me fight.

The door opens and Henry takes a step inside, looking between us. "What's going on?"

Jonny sneers at me, seething. "Just having words with your brother."

"What kind of words?" he asks. Butch comes in behind, and the two of them fill the kitchen so there's no room for anyone else.

Henry looks at me. I could sell Jonny out, tell Henry he's stirring shit up. I'm about to, the words are on my tongue, but then I don't.

All the guys in the kitchen will think I'm a pussy. I push my hat up so he can see my eyes. "I have a lead on some cars. I'm checking it out tomorrow," I say. "I was asking Jonny what he thought, if it was a good idea or not."

Jonny takes a step back; his fists unclench and he picks up his beer. Nodding, he pulls the tab on the can; the hiss of it opening cuts the tension. "Yeah, what he said." He walks out of the kitchen. I feel like I won a fight that never happened.

Henry takes a long breath. "Wheels come back yet?" he asks me. Butch brushes past him and gets a beer from the fridge. He holds it up and gives Henry a chin nod before he leaves the room. The other guys at the table go back to their pizza.

"Didn't see him."

He rubs a hand over his bristly hair and cracks his neck. "So, you got a plan."

It takes me a second to figure out what he's talking about. "Yeah," I say, "I'm going to check it out tomorrow."

Henry raises an eyebrow, his lids slipping down

as he looks at me. "You're taking it serious, what I said about initiative."

I nod.

"That's good. Jonny giving you a hard time?" he asks.

I shrug, but don't say anything. "Don't let him push you around." Easy for him to say, I think, looking at the size of his chest and how thick his neck is.

"Henry!" someone yells loud from the front door. "You got a visitor." The way they say it, I have to look because I worry it's the cops. But when I poke my head around the corner, I see it's not. It's Lester from Koob's rooming house.

I snort to myself in surprise and stay tucked in a corner.

My brother rolls his shoulders, cracking his neck. Lester didn't come on his own. Wheels is behind him, pushing him into the house. He sort of stumbles over the door, and I can tell he'd rather be anywhere but here.

Henry shakes his head. "Things aren't looking good for you," he says.

Lester moves his mouth, but no sound comes out.

"What's that?" Henry says, stepping closer.

Lester's eyes dart to him and then away. I can hear his breathing, even from across the room.

"Your brother and me had a deal. I did him a big favour. He said you'd be good for it. You *owe* me." Henry moves right up to him and breathes heavy in his face. Lester flinches.

"Give me till Friday. I-I get paid on Friday," he stammers and looks to the other guys like one of them might back him up.

Henry stares at him, his eyes narrowed, lips curled in a sneer. "Full payment Friday, or Wheels pays you another visit." Lester takes the hint and backs away. His hands are trembling and he's about to say something else when Henry turns away. Wheels shoves him and he trips down the steps.

I wait till Lester's a shadow on the sidewalk. "Hey, Henry," I say and walk across the room to talk to him. He collapses into a chair, and someone hands him a joint, already lit. "I know that guy. He lives in Koob's building."

Henry snorts. "What the hell do I care?"

I blink at him. Words swell in my chest. "He's a good guy."

Henry gives me one of those looks that makes me wish I kept my mouth shut and never said anything.

"Yeah? What's a good guy?" He takes a toke on the joint and passes it back to the guys on the couch. "Someone who owes you money? Someone who's been in jail? Am I a good guy, little bro?" His voice is all quiet and he's staring at me, so I have to answer.

"Yeah," I croak.

His lips stretch into a greasy smile. "That's right, cuz I'm your brother. So if I tell you Lester's *not* a good guy, you just fucking believe me. Got it?" His voice gets louder and I feel my heart beat against my ribs.

I nod and wait till he takes another long hit before I leave. My feet are heavy as I walk up the stairs. Machine-gun fire from a video game pounds through the walls and the house vibrates with it.

I open the door to a bedroom upstairs. Some guy's bare ass greets me. He's banging a girl on the bed and she's flopping around like a rag doll. I see her face.

Shit.

It's Roxy. I choke on my breath in surprise and shut the door quick. Too freaked out to say anything. The image burns itself on my brain.

I want to go back in and rip him off her, and I wonder if she saw me. I put my hand back on the doorknob. It's already cold like I never touched it. Pressing my ear to the door, I wait. Grunts. Squeaking bed springs, but no screams.

There's puke in my throat and I stumble into the bathroom. It burns, but nothing comes out. So I sit on the floor and pull my knees up to my chin. I don't want to go back out there. To Henry's jeers and the other guys with their dope and the fake good times.

I want to be with Koob and know someone's got my back.

But then I look around the bathroom. There's a brown sludge ring in the crapper and it smells like piss. I close my eyes for a second, because I'll gag if I keep looking at it. But when I open them, it's the same.

So I get up and go downstairs. I pull my hat so low that no one can see me, so low it almost covers my scar. I sit down on the couch and don't look at Henry. But I do take the joint when it gets handed to me.

Henry's leaning back in the chair; his eyes are closed and he's humming.

JAKUB

My eyes keep flicking back to the clock on the wall. I should be trying to follow what the teacher's droning on about, but I can't. All I can think about is Lincoln lurking in the trees outside.

The phone in my pocket vibrates. Our prearranged signal. I close my eyes and take a deep breath, willing myself to go through with this. I promised him. One car. Then, we're even.

I raise my hand and wince, holding my stomach. "I don't feel so good," I say when the teacher looks at me. I give her a pained look and go to her desk. She sighs and signs off on a hall pass. I nod my thanks. All the way to the parking lot doors, I keep my head down and shuffle slowly, in case a teacher stops me.

Halfway through second period, the parking lot is quiet. Guys have arrived for the morning, their cars shiny like candy in the lot. Link's across the parking lot. A row of cars separates us. He nods when he sees me lean against the building. All I have to do is keep watch, fake a coughing fit or something if someone comes by, I remind myself.

He sidles up to a Nissan Altima and bends his head over the driver-side door, and then disappears inside. It happens so quick that the door must have been left unlocked.

The door to the parking lot opens and three guys come out. Pressing myself against the wall, I duck my head, pretending to text. "Shit," I mutter under my breath. I glance up, praying they don't go toward Link and the Altima. Two stay together, but one veers off, heading in Link's direction. My heart speeds up. There's no way to warn Link, he's inside the car. If the kid sees him, that's it. Busted. I'm ready to shout something to get the guy's attention, make a fool of myself, anything to save my friend. But then I hear it. An engine roars to life.

The car is out of the lot in a minute, peeling toward the exit and onto the street. I stare after it, hardly believing Lincoln could get it going that fast. I'm about to turn back into the school when the guy walking on his own calls out to his friends, laughing. "Harris is the worst friggin' driver! Did you see how he took that corner?"

I wait for a second, but they don't know it wasn't their friend behind the wheel. It was mine.

My phone buzzes with a text. *Too easy,* it says. *I'll be back in an hour. Wait for my text.*

My head pounds. *We had a deal.* I text back.

I stare at the phone, waiting for a reply. Nothing. I thumb a *?* and wait. Teachers check these doors all the time. The hall pass was to go to the washroom, not hang around the student lot.

I hold the phone in my hand, willing it to vibrate with a message. But it stays blank, the screen glowing blue and empty.

If Link calls when I'm in class, I won't be able to answer and I sure as hell won't be able to leave again. He'll be on his own. Between now and then, the Harris kid could realize his car is missing. And even if he doesn't, it'll be bad timing so close to lunch. If Link comes back and someone spots him, a guy faking that he's a student, he'll get dragged inside to Father O'Shea. It wouldn't take much digging to figure out the connection between me and Link.

I yank open the doors, knowing I can't hang around any longer. If Link comes back, he's on his own.

I wait till third period bell rings and go to Mr. McGee's class. A history teacher who looks like he's lived through most of what he teaches. His eyes like piss holes in the snow zero in on any kid not paying attention. I cram my legs under the table and try to concentrate on what he's saying.

My breathing is finally settling into a normal rhythm when my phone rings. The tinny, robotic tune makes the class freeze. Phones in class are against the rules. Phones in McGeezer's class are suicide. Everyone looks around trying to locate the owner. I slide lower in my seat and fumble in my pocket, trying to turn it off.

It rings again. A catchy beat. Someone snickers. My face burns as the source of the sound is located.

All eyes are on me, including McGeezer's. "Please, Mr. Kaminsky, take your call. I'm sure it's important." His voice drips with sarcasm.

I shake my head. I don't know where the hang-up button is, or how to silence the ringing. I press buttons, trying to make it stop, but nothing works. All of a sudden, Lincoln's voice fills the classroom.

"Koob!" he yells.

My fingers tremble as I jab at the buttons. My hands are sweating with nerves. The phone slips to the floor. "That was too easy, man! I'm coming back. Meet me outside in fifteen minutes. Wheels is dropping me off. Koob? You there?"

McGeezer strides over and picks up the phone. He stands holding it out to me as I slouch lower in my seat. His gnarled hands wave it impatiently. I don't want the phone back.

"Can you hear me?" Link shouts into the silent classroom. "I'm coming back. We'll get one more."

Every kid in the class stares at me with a silent question. Get one more *what*? Finally, the call ends. Link hangs up and McGeezer drops the phone on my desk. It rocks on its hard, plastic shell. "Care to explain?" he asks.

I shut my eyes and press my lips together, praying that when I open them, no one will be looking at me.

But they are. Leaning out of their chairs and waiting to hear what I have to say. "It's not, ah, this isn't my phone," I stammer.

"Ahh, it's not your phone, Mr. Kaminsky. Yet, you had it on you, and based on the way you're acting, you're mortified we've all heard what the caller said. I would argue that it is indeed your phone. Mr. Creighton, would you agree?"

Tanner, blond and sun-tanned, like a surfer, spins around to face McGeezer. "Yes, sir," he says, quietly.

"I think, since your friend interrupted us, you should fill us all in on what he was talking about. Sounded very covert, didn't it? Please, Mr. Kaminsky, enlighten us." He mocks me, enjoying himself. I sit still, my silence defying him.

He glares at me, colour flaring in his saggy cheeks. "Leave, Mr. Kaminsky. Take your phone with you."

I stand up, a hot rush behind my eyes. I don't look at anyone as I make my way to the front of the class. "I'll be letting the bursary selection committee know about this," he says, loud enough for the whole class to hear.

By the time I get to the washroom, anger explodes from every limb. I fling my binder on the floor, and it bursts into a flurry of paper. I kick at the metal stall doors until my toes are numb, letting curses fly from my lips.

I pull the phone from my pocket. It was a stupid friggin' idea getting mixed up with Link and the Red Bloodz like this. Dropping it to the ground, I stamp on it till bits of metal and shattered plastic are all that's left. The SIM card pops out. I toss it in the toilet and flush it away.

Now what? I look around the washroom, taking deep breaths to calm myself. My fingers itch with anger, at Lincoln for dragging me into this and at McGeezer for humiliating me. At myself for saying yes.

Tucked into the pocket of my binder is a Sharpie, the black cap visible. I reach down to pick it up. A long expanse of mirror above the sink calls to me. A few swipes and McGeezer's nose, lumpy and engorged, appears, then his heavy brow, almost like a Neanderthal's, furrowed in anger. I make him decrepit, like an ogre, with small, beady eyes and hair growing out of his ears and nose. Standing back, I cap the pen and give the drawing a long, spiteful look. There's no mistaking who it is.

Link and I had a deal. One car, not two.

What happens when it goes sideways? What does Lincoln have left to lose? Nothing.

I could bust him myself. Tell Father O'Shea, blame everything on Lincoln. At least then Henry wouldn't want him.

But he's my friend. He saved my ass up on the building. I can't stab him in the back.

Squeezing my eyes shut, I think about what the right choice is. But there isn't one.

I pack up the papers on the floor and stuff the binder under my arm. I yank the washroom door open, slide into the hallway, and pray that I don't bump into a teacher. And that I can catch Lincoln before it's too late.

LINCOLN

Rat raises his eyebrows when I drive the Nissan through the back gate. He swings it closed and puts the padlock back on. "Nice." He whistles when I get out. "Where'd you get it?"

I don't want to tell him. Koob's school is a gold mine. But not for much longer. If I want to lift another one, I need to get back there before anyone figures out what's going on. Koob's left me messages on the cell. He's freaking out. Rookie.

Rat opens the hood and gets to work. One thing about that guy, he hustles.

I dial Koob's cell. It rings and I get impatient; my foot starts jittering. Then, the ringing stops, but no one says anything. "Koob!" I say. I can hear noises in the background. "That was too easy, man! I'm coming back. Meet me outside in fifteen minutes. Wheels is dropping me off. Koob? You there?"

The phone goes dead. Shit. I stand in the garage for a minute, breathing in the oil and gasoline, the grit that hangs in the air.

"Ha!" Rat laughs behind me and I turn. In his grimy hands, he's holding up the St. Bart's blazer. "You clever little shit!" he says.

A smile tugs at my lips, but I grab the blazer away from him and act pissed off. "You don't know shit," I say with a sneer.

"Heard you say you're going back out. Probably got a whole parking lot full of sweet rides for me, eh?" He laughs like he's not talking about cars. "Wheels is in the front." He nods to the office area, the legit part of the business.

I dial Koob's cell again. He's getting cold feet, same as I did the first time. Probably doesn't want me coming back, but I think about all those cars, ripe for the picking, and it's too tempting.

Wheels can drive me past the school; if there's heat, I'll leave.

I dial Koob's cell. It rings and rings, but he doesn't pick up. "Pussy," I mutter under my breath. In the front of the shop, Wheels is having a smoke. He tosses what's left of the cigarette on the ground, crushing it with his heel. "You ready?"

I nod.

"What about your guy inside. He's ready?"

"Yeah," I lie. "We're good." Henry told me to take some initiative, so that's what I'm doing. If I get another car, I'll split the money with Koob, let him see that lifting a couple of cars is worth it.

I get in the car and slouch low, so I can barely see out the window. The West End slides by as we head to St. Bart's.

"Drop me here," I say to Wheels, a block from the school. I'll walk the rest of the way. Wheels pulls over under some trees. They stretch over the street meeting at the top, like a friggin' archway.

"Text me," he grunts. "I'll wait here, then head back."

I nod and get out of the car. I wish I had my hat to pull down over my eyes. I keep my head bent, staring at the sidewalk, trying not to walk too fast.

I see the school and the parking lot. It's almost empty. A couple of kids are at the doors. I slow my steps even more, knowing I have to wait till they go inside. The Audi, white with lots of chrome, is sitting in the middle of the lot. My fingers itch at the thought of getting behind the wheel. And what Henry will do when I get to the chop shop with it.

The cell is heavy in my pants pocket. I pull it out and try Koob one more time. No answer. "Shit," I mutter, clenching my teeth.

There's more guys coming to the doors now, and I wonder if it's a break between classes. I need to lay low till they go back inside. I'm walking toward the front of the school and I can feel my heart beating faster. I didn't want to get this close. The other guys have ties and shirts on. Me, in just a T-shirt, will get noticed.

I scan the door for Koob, in case he's there but can't

answer his phone. Then a kid comes rushing out, a big guy. He runs to an empty spot in the lot. The place where the Nissan was. He looks around, spinning, waving his hands and shouting and swearing. Other guys run over, too; some look for their cars and some stand in the same empty spot with the guy.

There's sweat on my forehead. I pull my mouth in tight and force my feet to keep moving slow, even though I want to run and get the hell out of here. An Escalade drives past, turns into the driveway at the front of the school. A blond woman gets out and runs inside the building. The keys are in the ignition. I hear the engine humming, life still flowing through the car.

I look back once at the guys in the lot. They're looking around. Some are walking toward the sidewalk, close to where I am. And then, I see Koob. He's there, at the doors.

"Hey!" someone yells. I don't know if it's to me, but I hunch my shoulders under my jacket and speed up my steps. "Hey!" the voice says again. I turn quick and he's got a phone out, holding it in front of him.

The Escalade is close, if I run.

So I do. I bolt. Each slap of the pavement is a shout of guilt. There's more shouting behind me. I see the blond woman walking out of the school. We're heading to the same spot. The Escalade.

I get there first, yank open the door, and put it into drive before the door is even shut. Without looking at the lady, I step hard on the gas. I hear her scream. There's a noise behind me.

"Mommy!" A kid's in the backseat.

My heart hammers hard in my chest. Guys chasing me pound on the doors and windows, trying to catch a piece of the car before I get to the street. The kid's crying, her face red, and I don't know what to do. "Shut up!" I yell at her, because I can't think with all the noise.

There's guys on the sidewalk, holding out their phones, capturing my face. I get down low, so I can barely see over the steering wheel. The little girl is wailing. What am I gonna do with a kid? Dump her on the road?

The guys chasing me have fallen back, given up. I look in the rear-view mirror. There's a mob around the lady, but one lone guy stands on the sidewalk watching. Koob.

I drive fast, all over the road cuz I'm freaking out, trying to figure out what to do. The kid is shrieking, losing it that I'm taking her away from her mom. I run a red and there's a flash of a camera. There's too much heat. A white Escalade blazing down the street, with a kid in the back? Every cop in the city will be after me.

Shit! I won't make it to the chop shop in this thing. And the kid. I glance at her, real quick in the mirror. But instead of seeing her, all I see is me.

With a shout of frustration, I slam my palm on the steering wheel and pull onto a side street. I jump out and leave the Escalade running, the driver door hanging open, the girl's screams fill the air. Wheels's car is still there, idling.

He sees me coming and reaches over to open the passenger door. Before I'm even in the seat, he's pressing on the accelerator. My heart beats so hard, I can hear it. I peel the friggin' jacket off, bunch it up and toss it out the window.

"Do I want to know?" he asks.

I shake my head. "Just drive," I say and shut my eyes.

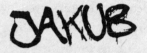

JAKUB

News of the car being stolen spreads through school quick. Father O'Shea comes over the PA and gives permission for all students with cars in the lot to check on them. Guys flood outside, even the ones without cars.

I go, too, slinking down the hallway and out the back doors. A crush of guys stands there. Harris is raging in his empty parking spot. A couple of the other football players huddle around him, consoling. A murmur of anger flows through the waiting crowd.

I don't see Link at first; I'm watching Harris.

"Who's that?" a voice says. And we all follow his raised arm, pointing at the sidewalk.

Other guys jostle to see, craning their necks. I do the same. Link slouches down the sidewalk, his blazer out of place with the rest of his outfit. No tie or shirt, baggy jeans, and old, beat-up running shoes. No one would mistake him for one of us.

Phones come out, grainy images of the stranger captured. More guys flood out of the building, the doorway thick with bodies. I move to the edge, closer to Link. *Run!* I think and feel the word jam itself in my throat.

His cover is blown. "Run, Link," I whisper under my breath.

On some silent cue, the guys swell toward him, swarming across the grass. Link starts running. Seconds later, a white Escalade careens onto the street, chased by guys with flailing arms and jackets flapping behind them. They shout, reach out for the truck, their effort futile because Link presses on the gas and leaves them in his dust.

"Stop!" I yell, the same as the others. *Link, just stop.*

And then a woman screams. "My baby!" she howls. "He's got Kennedy!"

My stomach drops. A kid. He's taken a car with a kid in it. *Link.* I shake my head. *What have you done?*

The lady who owns the Escalade starts screaming; her uncontrollable sobs fill the air. I've seen her before, at the Nearly New shop. Tanner, the kid from McGeezer's class, comes outside, and I realize it's his mom's car that was just stolen. His little sister inside of it. His mom is still screaming for someone to call the cops. Tanner puts an arm around her, protectively, and pulls out his phone. My gut's churning so bad, I think I'll shit my pants right here.

They refuse to go inside, so none of us want to, either. We stand milling around until the wail of a cop car can be heard.

"Give them privacy," the teachers say, herding us back into the school.

"What kind of an asshole steals cars? One with a kid in it?" one guy says, shaking his head.

A desperate one, I think.

But the morning is a write-off. No one can concentrate, not even the teachers. If Link still has the Escalade, he'll have taken it to the chop shop. Did he ditch the kid on the road somewhere? But he might have bailed, left the kid in the truck and taken off, too freaked out to drive it through the city.

If I'd said something an hour ago, none of this would have happened. Tanner's little sister would be safe. Link wouldn't be a grainy photo on thirty kids' phones.

Guilt gnaws at me. It radiates through my skin and I duck down, hunching in my desk, terrified that someone will notice.

Finally, Father O'Shea's voice, calm and steady, comes on the PA.

"The Creighton family would like to thank everyone for their prayers. The child in the stolen car has been found and is unharmed." A cheer goes through the class. I see my teacher raise her eyes and murmur a quick prayer of thanks. I do the same, but not just for the little girl. "I'm sure a full report will be on the news tonight. In the meantime, please respect the family's privacy and resist the urge to speculate. The police are doing their best to resolve the situation."

Guys around me mutter their revenge fantasies. I sink lower in my seat, wishing I could crawl under it. I didn't press on the gas pedal or drive it out of the lot, but Link wouldn't have either if it wasn't for me.

Link is falling, slipping out of my grasp and tumbling somewhere I can't reach him.

When I see someone sitting on the front steps, I think it's Lincoln, and my stomach lurches because I don't know what I'll say to him. I'm too mad to think straight. The events of the day have bled into a pulpy mess. But it's not Lincoln. It's Lester, hunched over, smoking. He raises his head in greeting when I turn up the sidewalk.

"Hey," I say. He has a beer between his feet and a couple of empties piled up behind him. "Day off?"

"Something like that," he mumbles. He takes a sip from the can and stares across the street. Pouches of skin under his eyes are pronounced against the gauntness of his face.

"You okay?"

Lester runs a hand over his greying hair. For as long as I've known him, he's worn it pulled back into a skinny rat-tail. "I'm leaving," he says. I move closer to make sure I heard him right.

"What?"

"Got to get away. Owe some guys money."

"Shit." I let my backpack drop to the ground and sit down beside him. "When are you leaving?"

"Tomorrow, or the next day. Wanna say goodbye to the guys at Fenty's and then I'll take off."

"Did you tell Laureen?"

He sucks on his teeth and shakes his head. "Not yet. Don't want to. I'm paid up for rent, but I'd rather just sneak out in the night." He turns to me. "Maybe you could do it? Tell her I got a job on the rigs, or something. Had to leave right away."

"Nah, man. That's not right. She'll want to say good-bye to you."

Lester sighs. "Guess you're right. Kind of chicken shit, to do it my way."

"How much is it?" I ask. "The money. How much do you owe?"

Lester's eyes flare. "It's my fucking no-good brother. It's his debt I'm on the hook for."

We sit together on the stairs watching traffic on the street go past.

He pops the tab on another beer. "Look at that." He nods at my backpack. "I don't know if I ever opened a book when I was your age." He gives a rueful laugh. "Guess that explains things, eh?"

We sit quiet for a few minutes. A dog down the street barks as someone walks by. "You're really going?"

He purses his lips, his whole body rocking with a nod. "No choice."

"Not gonna be the same around here." I hold up my hand and he clasps it in his.

His mouth twitches, but he covers it up with a draw on his smoke. "Thanks, kid."

Laureen's phone is in my hand. I stare at it a few minutes before pressing the numbers, trying to work out what

I'll say to Lincoln if he answers. Finally, I just dial and hope that when I hear his voice, I'll just know.

"Yeah." Link's voice echoes into the receiver.

"It's me," I say. Silence on the other end. "We need to talk."

He snorts on the other end. "About how you bailed on me?"

With a groan of frustration, I try again. "Look, man." I lower my voice, cupping my hand over the receiver. "Things went sideways. A teacher took my phone. We almost got busted."

"I was the one outside," he hisses. "Your friggin' faggot friends were after me!"

Running a hand through my hair, I hear him breathing on the other end of the phone. "You took a car *with a kid in it!*"

There's noise in the background, laughing and talking.

"Where are you?" I ask.

"Doesn't matter."

"Can we meet at the park?"

Link gives a long exhale, thinking about it. "I'll be there in fifteen."

I hang up and know that I'll have to paint tonight. A car with the Red Bloodz dagger stabbed through the hood. I grab my sketchbook and do a rough outline of the idea before I lose it. The list of cars Link wanted to steal is on the other side of the paper. A few sheets away, the one of him and Dad climbing the stairs on the first day of school. *Where's that kid?* I wonder. How could Henry and his gang pull him away so quickly?

But I know the answer. It's hanging inside the apartment on a shitty wire hanger. The day I got accepted to St. Bart's was the day Henry's grip got so tight on Link he couldn't escape.

LINCOLN

I stare anywhere but at Koob as he walks toward me. When he slides onto the bench, I inch away, but I don't think he notices. At least, he pretends not to.

"That didn't go down how I thought it would," I say. I try to stay cool, but inside I'm choking on all the things I want to tell him.

"No shit," he says, his eyes bugging out.

I grit my teeth and stare at the garbage can.

"Shit, Link. If you'd been caught! That was kidnapping." He hisses the words at me. "You got away with one. You didn't need to come back."

He doesn't know what it's like, trying to impress the guys at the clubhouse. I want to wipe the stupid look off Jonny's face for once, make him see I'm not just some punk-ass little brother. "I was showing initiative," I mumble. "And where the hell were you?" I say, turning on him. "Doing fuck-all while those guys almost caught me!"

Koob gets in real close and flicks the brim of my hat, tipping it back so he can see my eyes. "I *told* you not to come back. I was in class. A teacher took my phone. I could have been expelled just for that, never mind stealing a fucking car!"

I let out a deep breath and sort of laugh. It was close with those guys after me. If that Escalade hadn't been there … I shake my head thinking about what would've happened.

But Koob doesn't think it's funny. He grabs my jacket in his hands and pushes me back hard against the bench. "You almost got me kicked out, you asshole. Why are you laughing?" His eyes are narrowed and he looks more pissed than I've ever seen him.

I push him back and he lets go, but we're both on our feet. "Who gives a fuck about a school?"

"I do!"

I snort at him, disgusted. "Used to be a time when you had priorities. Me, your dad. Where'd that guy go? You're turning into one of them."

"What about you? What are you turning into? Kidnapping little kids, stealing cars. What's next? Huh? What's Henry's next big plan for you?"

I don't like him talking about Henry. Blood rushes to my head, and my hands curl into fists before I even know what I'm doing. "He's looking out for me," I snarl.

"Bullshit! He's using you." Koob's backing up, circling me. "All this is about money. He's got you doing all his dirty work. He doesn't give a fuck about what happens to you. If you get caught, go to juvie, he'll just find some other dumb shit to do the work for him."

Koob's never called me dumb before. It knocks the wind out of me hearing what he really thinks about me.

From the street, a car with a thumping bass makes me turn and look. A familiar low-rider with tinted windows rolls past. It stops on the other side of the chain-link fence. The window rolls down. Henry pushes his sunglasses, black wraparounds, to the top of his head and stares at me.

I can't let him see me back down from a fight.

I take a swing at Koob. It almost catches him in the gut, but he jumps away too quick. Both of us breathe hard, waiting for the next move. He comes at me and grabs me around the waist so we both go down on the ground. He's on top at first, shouting at me, spit flying out of his mouth, but I can't hear him because all I'm thinking about is that Henry might hear him and we'll both get a pounding from him. I have to shut him up.

I raise a leg behind him and kick. He rolls off to the ground and then I'm on top. I give him two good ones to the face and blood pours out of his nose. "Fuck!" he yells, holding his face. My hand hurts, but I stand up.

Henry's still there. I don't have to turn around because I can feel him, like a shadow. I collect spit in my mouth and blow a wad at Koob. It lands beside him. "Fuck you!" I say real loud. I turn and walk to the car.

He groans and staggers up, but I'm already walking out of the park.

When I slam the car door shut, I'm breathing hard. My hand throbs.

I'm waiting for Henry to say something, but he stays silent till we get to a stoplight. Then he turns around, eyeing me. "What were you doing with him?"

"Why does it matter?" I ask.

He narrows his eyes. "Cuz it does."

"He played me. I had to show him he can't mess with me no more."

Henry snorts. "You call *that* showing him? You gave him two pansy punches and walked away. You should've *finished* him."

I seethe from the back seat.

Rat laughs beside him. A nasally whine that makes me grit my teeth.

"You're a joke," Henry says.

"Go to hell," I mutter.

"What did you say?" he asks, leaning back so hard in the seat, I think it's going to snap.

"I said to go to hell." Bolder now, I say it louder. He thinks he can boss me around, treat me like shit and get away with it. One muscular hand reaches out for me and grabs a fistful of T-shirt.

"Don't you ever talk like that to me again. I don't care who you are. I will beat you to a pulp. I will show you how you send a message. Got it?" His eyes are like firebrands. I try to nod, but my body is frozen. He's looking at me like he could snap my neck if he felt like it. When he finally lets go, I fall back against the back seat.

"Hanging out with that kid, that's what made you soft." He's watching me from the rear-view mirror, his mouth set in a disappointed scowl. "We got to toughen

143

you up, little brother. See if you really got what it takes to run with us."

I have a dream that night that I'm drowning. The muck of the river bottom makes my feet stick. The water swirls around me and I'm screaming cuz I can't move and the water's getting higher. When I wake up, I'm sweating and my heart's pounding cuz the nightmare felt so real. I kick off the sheets twisted around my ankles and lie on the mattress, trying to remember why I'm here and not at my house.

Then it all comes back to me and I feel like I'm drowning all over again.

JAKUB

I can't tell Dad what really happened. My nose swells and I wonder if it's broken. I'm too mad at Link to notice how bad the rest of my face is throbbing until I get in front of the apartment door. Drops of blood stain the front of my shirt. If Dad's awake, he's going to freak out.

I try to sneak in, quiet. He's in the corner of the couch, reading a book. One light beside him makes a circle just big enough for the pages to be seen. The rest of the apartment is dark. Perfect.

"Where were you?" he asks, looking up. The bad lighting camouflages my face. I keep my head down and go to the washroom.

"At the park. I was supposed to meet Link."

He doesn't say anything. My face feels like it's going to burst through the skin. When I splash water on my face, a thin stream of pink trickles out of one nostril.

In the kitchen, I put some ice cubes in a towel and hold it to my face. Instantly, it feels better and I sigh. Dad's off the couch and hobbling toward me. "What happened?"

"Got jumped," I lie. "On my way to the park."

"Who?" He wants to know. His eyes bulge in anger.

I shrug. "Don't know. Didn't see them."

He holds my elbow and leads me to the couch. "Dad," I say, shirking him away. "I'm fine. It's not a big deal."

"*Pfft*. Not a big deal! It is a big deal." We both fall to the couch, a spring creaking against the weight. He pulls the ice pack away and inspects my nose, shaking his head and muttering in Polish. "Where was Lincoln in all this?"

"He never showed. Probably with his brother." Bitterness creeps into my voice.

"You see now why I wanted you to go to St. Bartholomew's?"

I shut my eyes and nod.

"You're a good boy, Jakub. You deserve a chance."

His voice swirls in the background as I lean back against the worn, nubby upholstery and wait till the throbbing in my face subsides. Lincoln went too far this time. Whatever history we had together is just that: history. From now on, my life is with St. Bart's.

LINCOLN

"Where are we going?" I ask once. The other guys, Wheels and Rat, throw me looks, so I shut up. No one tells me anything. They just bark at me with orders like "Get in the car" and "Get me a beer." Wheels turns the music up so loud, no one can talk anyway. My knuckles are split. I touch the still-soft scab and wonder how Koob's doing, how bad I hurt him last night. *Stop caring*, I tell myself. My loyalty's with Henry and the Red Bloodz. Koob's nothing to me.

We stop in front of Fenty's Bar. A few people hang out on the corner, leaning against the building. Only Rat gets out. Henry and I stay in the car as Wheels pulls it around the back, into the alley. I try to catch someone's eye so they'll fill me in, but no one bites.

Wheels kills the music and my ears ring from the silence. My brother cracks his knuckles, opening and closing his fist. I swallow hard, watching him. My foot starts to tap, rocking up and down against the floor in the back seat.

The engine is still running when Henry gets out of the car and goes around to the trunk. I stay sitting in the back as he pulls something out. The lid slams shut and I jump. When he comes around to my window, his jaw is clenched so tight I can see the bones sticking out through his cheeks. He taps on the window. A signal for me to join him. I want to stay in the car, cower against the back seat, but I can't.

I get out slow, pull my hat down low so he can't see my eyes. The alley stinks like sour beer, the cement sticky with it. Wheels reverses out of the alley, flinging pellets of gravel from under the tires. Henry's nostrils flare open and he rolls his shoulders. I look at the tire iron in his hands and he glares at me, his eyes hooded and mean, a warning to toughen up.

A grey door with the words "Fenty's Bar" half scratched off opens.

Lester walks out. Rat's behind him, his pointy face twisted in a scowl. Lester stumbles; he's been drinking. His eyes roll from Rat to Henry. He tries to go back inside, but Rat moves in front of the door and pushes him toward Henry.

"I told you I'd get your money," he mumbles, staggering.

"When? After you took off?" Henry walks up close to him. "You're too stupid to even keep that quiet. Think you can dick us around?" Henry yells, spraying Lester with spit. Lester doesn't wipe it away, just keeps his head bent, staring at the ground.

"I told you, man —" He's desperate, his words jumbled. But Henry doesn't let him finish. At a chin nod,

Rat drags Lester to the other side of the alley, behind a dumpster. Lester resists, kicking at the ground until one of his work boots comes off.

"No one messes with us," Henry says.

Lester's bony and his face is weathered, like a piece of wood that's been battered by the sun and wind. His eyes are wide and terrified; he knows what's coming. He sees me, standing behind Henry. His face twists with surprise. "Lincoln!" he shouts, like I might be able to help him. "Lincoln?" I turn away. My gut aches for him and I feel puke rising in my throat.

Henry's in my face. He grabs my hand and slaps the tire iron in it. It's heavy and thin, and I know what he wants me to do with it. What people usually do with a weapon: break a knee, smash in a skull, crack ribs.

My fingers barely curl around it. I don't want it in my hand.

"You said you wanted in. Show me." I look between him and Lester. I freeze, staring at the weapon in my hands.

I hesitate too long. Henry snorts with disgust. "I knew it." He goes to grab the tire iron, but I jerk it away. I tighten my grip and take a step toward Lester.

"Please, Lincoln! Please. Don't! Aw, man, come on!" He shakes his head and mutters, begging and swearing.

"Shit," I swear under my breath. I hold the tire iron out, ready to whack him with it. Henry's breathing is loud and close. He's impatient, us being in the alley for so long.

I close my eyes and take a swing. It lands across Lester's arm and back. He clutches at where I hit him and moans. "Again!" Henry yells in my ear, so loud it drowns out Lester. Tears blur my eyes and I blink them away.

Lester's just sitting there. He's not trying to run or nothing. "Get up!" I want to yell at him. *Don't make this so easy.* The next swing catches him in the leg. "You're not even trying!" Henry says and cuffs me on the head so my hat falls off.

"Get up!" Henry yells at Lester and kicks him in the leg. Lester howls with pain and grabs where I hit him. He scuttles to the wall, his eyes wide with fear. He's pissed himself. A dark stain grows on his pants. "Again, you pussy!" Henry hisses to me.

I swing the tire iron like a baseball bat. Squeezing my eyes shut, I can feel it come down hard on his side. When I open my eyes, Lester's writhing, mouth open wide in soundless pain. I stand back, my breath in hot pulses.

Lester starts moaning, low and soft like a dying animal. I did that, I think. I can taste puke. I shut my lips tight, swallowing it.

Henry looks at Lester like he's a bug he can crush. He rips the tire iron from my hand and whacks it across Lester's body, fast and vicious. I turn away until I hear Henry stop. Lester's not moving. Henry's breathing hard, and then his boot is raised over Lester's head.

Someone shouts, "No!" but between the sound of bones cracking and the spurt of blood, I don't know it's me till my throat aches from it.

"Shit!" Rat says, kind of in awe, and takes a step back. He looks at Henry.

I start to shake.

Henry's already moving away, taking huge backward strides away from Lester. "Let's go," he says, and even he sounds freaked out.

Lester is on the ground, a pool of blood spreading on the pavement. I take a step closer, making sure I'm seeing it right.

Rat grabs my arm and spins me away. "You nuts?" His eyes are big and scared.

He yanks on my arm, and we hustle out of the alley to Wheels and the waiting car. Henry stashes the tire iron in the trunk and then jumps in the front seat. Rat and me get in the back. I'd pass out if I wasn't sitting down.

Wheels looks at us, waiting for someone to tell him what happened. "Go," Henry says. No one says anything, and then Henry turns the music up louder.

I slide low in my seat and go to pull my hat down, but it isn't there.

"My hat," I yell.

Henry turns all the way in his seat. I can feel Rat's eyes on me, too.

"It's back there." I put my hand on the door handle, ready to get out.

Wheels puts the car in drive. Tires spin on gravel and cracked pavement. I fall back against the seat.

"But, my hat!"

"Too bad, man!" Rat laughs. Only it's not a real laugh, it's the kind that's forced. His eyes are round and glassy, and I bet he wants to puke, too.

I shut my eyes. *It's got my name in it,* I want to tell them. They'd go back and get it if they knew that.

But going back into the alley, seeing Lester's broken body, the blood. I can't do it. The words get stuck in my throat.

The car's beat-up suspension creaks over potholes. I gag and try to look out the window, pulling the red bandana low, hiding under it. Wheels blows past a stop sign. Home is close. I think about opening the car door and rolling out, like how they do in the movies.

Henry looks at me in the rear-view mirror. His toughness can't cover up the desperate look in his eyes. "You're not gonna puss out on me, are you?"

I can't look at him. "My hat —" I say and my voice cracks, so I don't say anything else.

Henry takes a long breath. "Drop him on the corner," he shouts to Wheels over the music. "He needs some air."

I think I might cry with relief when Wheels pulls to the curb and I stumble out. The walk to my street is only a block away, but it stretches so far in front of me, I wonder if I can make it because all of sudden, I realize we killed Lester.

I stumble, dragging my feet over the cracks in the sidewalk. I want to crawl into my bed, turn off the lights, and never wake up. Never talk to anyone again because what if I spill everything that just happened? What if the truth spurts out of me like a cut artery and I can't make it stop?

Everything is so jumbled in my head. I need a place dark and quiet to think. I'm almost at my house when I see Koob waiting on the front steps.

He raises his hand when he sees me, like nothing's changed.

I almost collapse from the weight of it, because everything's changed.

JAKUB

All day at school, every time I touched my nose I was reminded of Link. How he looked when he took the swings at me, his face contorted with anger. That wasn't the guy I knew.

Kids at school were still talking about the carjacking. Harris wasn't hurting from it, though. He drove up in a new car that other guys stood around admiring. News crews hung around the perimeter of the school grounds, trying to get eye-witness reports about what happened. The teachers told us to ignore them. *You want a story*, I thought to myself. *I could give them a real story: gangs, violence, all the things that sell papers.*

I thought about the little girl in the back of the Escalade. How scared she must have been. And Link, probably freaking out once he realized he wasn't alone. They were the same, the two of them. Link was being held by his brother, the same as the kid. Neither one of them wanted to be there, but there was no way out.

Maybe he'll listen to reason now. I came down hard on him last night, forcing him into a corner. I know how things are with him and Henry. I should've stayed cool.

I'll go to Link's place after school, I promise. See if I can make up for yesterday. Show him some of the new pieces I want to do. Maybe if we can paint tonight, things will feel like normal again. I'll have my friend back.

Lincoln's chain-link gate clangs shut behind me. One winter, we poured water on the latch and watched it freeze. For a few days, everyone had to jump over the four-foot fence to get inside his yard, until his mom made him chip the ice off with a screwdriver.

I knock on the door, trying to remember if the doorbell has ever worked. Lincoln's mom comes to answer it. Her long hair is slicked back into a ponytail. "Hi, Jakub." She doesn't open the screen door and it stands between us. One of Lincoln's little cousins walks across the hall behind her in a diaper, pulling a noisy toy. There's always kids coming and going at Lincoln's house. It's hard to keep track of them.

"Lincoln home?" I ask.

She shakes her head. "Hasn't been around much since his brother came home."

Her words are like a quick slice of a knife blade, unintentional but painful. "If he comes by, can you tell him I'm looking for him?"

She nods. One of the kids starts to cry, a half-hearted whine. She closes the door and shouts at him to be quiet.

I linger for a minute on the front porch. A stroller sits to the side, sun-faded and dirty, with a ripped seat. No point in hanging around waiting for him, but I'm not in a hurry to leave, either.

There's a guy on the sidewalk, walking real slow with his head hanging down. At first glance, I think it's an old man, but then I see it's Link. He pauses at the gate to his house, like he isn't sure if he should open it or not.

"Hey," I say, walking toward him. There's a flicker of relief in my gut, like a knot has been loosened.

His head stays down. But with no hat on, I can see his chin trembling.

I open the gate and he moves past me, like a ghost.

"Link?" I say. "What happened?"

He shakes his head, his lips quivering cuz he's trying to hold back tears. He sits down in the middle of his yard and covers his face with his hands. I watch in shock because I've never seen Lincoln cry. Ever.

I crouch beside him on the grass. Helpless. "What the hell? What happened?" Flashes of Henry, his gang, the power they have. What had they done to him?

"I think he's dead," he whimpers.

I stare at him, not ready to react. "Who?"

Tears drip onto his shirt.

"Lester!" He wipes an arm across his face, smearing a wet line of snot on his sleeve. He leans over and gags, retching till he pukes.

"Lester?" I ask, sure I haven't heard right. "From my building?"

Lincoln nods.

"What happened?"

But Link can't answer. He shakes his head and stares at me, helpless.

"Link!" I say and grab his shoulders. "What happened?"

"They got him in an alley. Beat him up. I think," he sputters through a choking sob, "they killed him."

I don't need to ask who.

"The money," I breathe. Lester owed it to the Red Bloodz. "You were there?"

Link gives a miserable nod, his eyes shiny with tears. "I'm one of them now. I got no choice."

He starts to cry angry tears, ripping off the bandana and pulling at his hair.

"Where is he?" He doesn't answer, so I grab his arms, forcing him to look at me. "Where?"

He takes a deep breath, trying to pull himself together. "The alley behind Fenty's." Link looks at me, desperate, like a trapped animal. "My hat's there." He squeezes his eyes shut, digging the heel of his palms into them.

I stand up on shaky legs.

Link raises a tear-stained face to me. "Where are you going?"

"I gotta see for myself. He might have faked going down," I tell him. "Go, get inside." He doesn't argue. Stumbling up the front steps, he lets the screen door slam shut.

I take a breath and leave Link's yard, shutting the gate tight behind me. The metal latch clangs, ringing in my ears as I walk away.

I walk quickly, keeping my head down, trying not to think what I might find when I get there. Fenton Avenue is a short street that dead-ends at an old candy factory. At night, it crawls with girls looking to make some money and druggies in need of a fix, or customers from Fenty's Bar. I put up my hood and roll my shoulders back, trying to look as tough as possible, on guard for anyone looking to jump me.

There's two dumpsters side by side halfway down the alley, a few disintegrating cardboard boxes that never made it to the garbage, and a couple of pallets stacked against the wall of a building. A light over the back door of the bar make glass from smashed bottles and syringes sparkle at my feet. I take a few steps in, craning my neck to see Lester and hoping, praying, that I won't.

And I don't. All I find is Link's flat-brim hat, lying on the ground a couple feet in front of me. With a relieved sigh, I pick it up and spot a work boot. Black, it blends into the grime of the alley. Was it Lester's? I move closer and look beside the dumpster.

There, in a heap, is Lester. He isn't moving. A bluish tinge paints his lips and around his eyes. Half-open, they stare blank into the alley. I freeze, waiting for his chest to move. There's a pool of blood under his head.

Hot tingles spread over my body. I should go. I should call the cops.

What would they say? Would they want to know why I was in this alley? What if they put it together, figure out Red Bloodz is to blame? If Henry discovers I found Lester, he'll know Lincoln told me. I can't do that to Lincoln.

Or myself.

I wait, praying Lester's chest will rise and fall, ignoring the colour of his skin, the blood on the ground, his expressionless face. But, it doesn't. I hear sirens, dim, but getting louder. I back away, making sure the hood is up, covering my face. I hold Link's hat tight in my hand. Zigzagging through alleys, I'm blocks away before I hear the sirens stop.

LINCOLN

Mom's on the phone with Dustin's head on her lap when I walk in. He's watching TV and one of my auntie's kids is eating Cheerios off the floor. She looks at me but doesn't say anything, so I go up to my room and shut the door.

I'm sweating and shivering and want to lie down, but I'm afraid to. I pace and squeeze my eyes shut, wishing I could just wake up. "Please," I beg, "make it be a nightmare." But it isn't, and now I'm going to live with what I did forever.

Lester's dead.

I told Koob.

It hits me like a punch to the gut. I shouldn't have done that. Henry will kill me, too, if he knows I said something. I start to sweat all over again.

"Link?" Dustin's at the door now, standing in front of me with his natty old blanket, shredded and dirty.

There's smears of food on his face and he's wearing a monster truck shirt that used to be mine.

"What?"

He stands at the door and doesn't say anything.

"What?" I shout and he jumps and runs down the stairs. I brought this into the house, all the shit that comes with Henry. It's like a sickness and I can't poison Dustin with it, too.

I grab a duffle bag from the closet. There's a dresser in my room, an old wooden one with chipped paint and sticky drawers. None of them close right. On hot days, they don't open right, either. I yank at them, shaking the drawer till it comes loose.

I don't hear Mom come up the stairs, so when she's standing in my doorway, I'm kind of surprised, but pretend that I'm not. "Where're you going?" she asks, looking at the bag on the bed. She pushes her glasses up on her nose.

"What do you care? You kicked me out." I toss some T-shirts onto the bed, and another pair of jeans.

She doesn't say nothing, just watches me. Makes me feel worse, having her there. Tears start to prickle behind my eyes again. I wish she'd go away.

"You don't have to go." She's wearing shorts, and the flesh of her legs, washed-out brown, takes up most of the doorway.

It's too late, I want to tell her. It's like when water gets sucked down a drain. Stuffing a finger in to stop it won't do any good. The water still slips away.

I grab a hat from the bottom of the closet. Doesn't fit

as good as my other one, but I pull it low over my eyes.

She looks at me when I squeeze past her in the door-way. For a second, we're pressed together, the door frame forcing us close. "What do you want me to tell Dustin?"

I frown at her. "Whatever you told me when Henry left."

There are streaks on her glasses, but when she stares at me, her eyes are hurt. I can't talk because of the lump in my throat. The sound of my footsteps on the stairs fills up the house where our voices should be.

Dustin's on the couch, rubbing his blanket against his cheek. I hold up my fist for a bump, burying grease-stained fingernails in my palm. His little hand taps mine. "Where're you going?" he asks.

"To a friend's."

"You coming back?" He looks at the bag I'm carrying.

"Yeah. I'll be back soon," I lie. I take a marker and write my cell number on his blanket. "You know how to use the phone, right? If you need me, call this number."

Dustin nods, all serious, and I wish I didn't have to go, but I do.

Mom's still upstairs, so I let the door slam loud on purpose behind me, so she'll know I'm gone.

JAKUB

I crush Lincoln's hat in my hand, squeezing it hard and wishing I could wring out the bad.

My stomach lurches for him. He crossed a line. There's no going back now.

If there are cars on the street, I don't hear them. People pass me, but I'm like a zombie, vacant with shock. Lester's face settles in the back of my mind, haunting me.

I walk past St. Mary's. The front door is open, like an invitation. Rows of candles are lit on the altar, small twinkling lights in red glass under the statue of the Virgin Mary.

Father Dom is there, walking the aisles, straightening the songbooks. "Jakub!" he greets me, but one look at my face and his expression changes. "Come," he says and steers me to his office. "Is it your father?"

I shake my head. "No." His eyes go to my hands and Link's hat.

He gives a sigh, like he knew this day was coming. With the door closed, Father Dom takes off his robe and hangs it on a hook. Pulling a sweatshirt over his T-shirt, he looks like any ordinary guy.

Father Dom points to a chair and I sit down, waiting for him to do the same. "Tell me," he says, pulling up a chair and giving me his full attention.

It's hard to look at Father Dom, never mind tell him.

"If someone did something really bad, like really bad, would you have to tell the police?"

"It depends. Are they going to do it again?"

I saw the look on Link's face, the way he stumbled and puked. He's not a killer. I shake my head. "No."

"Is anyone's life in danger?" Mine. If Henry finds out I know.

"No."

"Confessions are kept secret. They are between me, you, and God. Whatever you tell me will not leave this room." I've heard this speech before, but nod anyway. He leans forward, waiting.

"Lester's dead. He was murdered in the alley behind Fenty's Bar."

Father Dom sits back in his chair. He closes his eyes, crosses himself, and mutters a quick prayer. When he opens his eyes, they are dark and intense. His mouth is set in an angry, thin line, and I lean away from him. He looks at the hat in my hands. "And you know who did this?"

I nod. A wave of nausea rolls through me.

"Jakub!"

He's never shouted at me before and I jump. My nerves are already fried and I start to tremble.

"You need to go to the police!"

"I can't." My voice cracks.

"This is *murder*," he hisses.

I run my finger along the brim of Lincoln's hat. The band inside is stained yellow with sweat. For ten years, we've been like brothers. I can't betray him. Even if the cops only go after Henry, Lincoln will know I'm the one who talked.

"Who? Who did it?"

"I can't tell you," I say, miserably. "And I can't tell the cops!"

"Why not?"

I stay silent, wishing I'd walked past the church instead of coming inside. He glowers at me, disappointment etched into every wrinkle and jowl. I squeeze my eyes shut. "What do I do?" I whisper.

"You know what you have to do! If Lester was killed, and you know who did it, you have to go to the police. Not telling them makes you guilty, too."

Right and wrong are tangled together. I can't rat out my friend. If I do, the Red Bloodz will come after me, maybe Dad, too.

Lester's body flashes in my mind. They beat him to death and watched as the life leaked out of him, and then left him in an alley like a piece of garbage. He didn't deserve that. What Henry did wasn't just wrong, it was evil. Telling the cops means he'll go away. I'll have my friend back.

Or would I? Things would never be like they used to be, not with this between us. Not if Link knew I helped send Henry away again.

Thoughts twist themselves in my mind, pulling into a knot. There's no easy way. No matter what I do, someone gets hurt.

Father Dom lets out a deep exhalation. A painting of Jesus with long, flowing hair surrounded by a halo of light hangs on the wall behind him. I feel him staring at me, his eyes boring into me.

"Is it Lincoln?" he asks.

I hesitate. He knows I wouldn't protect anyone else. My eyes go to the hat crumpled in my hands. "Yeah." My voice is a choked whisper.

He gets up, goes around his desk, picks up his phone, and holds it in front of my face. "You know what you have to do."

There's an ache deep in my gut. It's too much, the weight of betraying my friend. I shake my head. "I can't," I say and turn to leave without looking at him.

"Jakub!" His red-faced shout follows me as I leave his office. It echoes off the walls of the church and rings in my ears when I push open the heavy wooden doors to the outside.

LINCOLN

Henry eyes me up and down when I walk into the clubhouse with the duffle bag. "You moving in?"

I don't answer. Upstairs, I pick the room at the top of the stairs, the one Roxy brought me into the first night I met her. I slam the door with my foot and toss my bag in the corner. The mattress is on the floor and the blanket is half-chewed by mice, but I don't care. I lie down and stare at the ceiling, remembering the first time I lay here with Roxy, how that felt, and I wonder if I'll ever feel that way again.

And it's Henry's fault. Koob was right. I never should have gotten mixed up with him, but now it's too late and I'm in this.

Bang, bang, bang. Someone's hammering on the door. I don't even remember locking it. "Link, open up." It's Henry.

I don't answer.

"Don't make me bust the door in." It's not a threat because I know he will.

"What?" I say when I open the door.

His nostrils flare and I think he's gonna yell at me for being a wuss. I stare back at him and scowl. "The first one's rough," he says. "And you knew him. Makes it hard." He takes a breath and nods at me. "But you manned up, did what you needed to do. The important thing now is to put it behind you. Forget it happened."

I look down at his boots. He cleaned them; the leather's shiny, no dirt or blood left to tie him to the crime.

"You wanted this, remember? 'Give me a chance.'" He imitates me with a high-pitched whine. I hang my head because he's right. "The guys are downstairs. You gotta come down so they know you're cool."

I don't have a choice. I follow him to the kitchen. A bare bulb hangs over the table, making shadows on the dreary, cracked walls. The old fridge hums and the faucet leaks. Wheels, Rat, and Butch are at the kitchen table. The guys look at me, anxious. No one says anything. There's a half-empty bottle of Jack Daniel's on the table. Rat stands up and takes a glass from a cupboard. He rinses it out and puts it down in front of me, water droplets puddling under it.

Butch pours some Jack into it and nods for me to drink up. It'll burn going down my throat. Henry's eyes are on me, not hooded and lazy, but threatening. Butch pours a glass for himself and holds it up. "This fucking life," he says and raises his glass. The other guys do the same. They wait for me.

"This fucking life," I mutter and put the glass to my lips. I wince at the taste, the feeling of it when I swallow, and slam the glass down, nodding for another one.

JAKUB

"This is incomplete, Mr. Kaminsky." McGeezer's beady eyes glare at me. I take his criticism silently, not sure if I should look away or not. My eyes are gritty from lack of sleep. "I don't care if you have an excuse. You will finish it in detention after school."

My excuse thrums in my skull, incessant. *I saw a dead body yesterday.* Will that truth get me out of detention? What if I tell him everything? That I saw Lester lying in the alley, that I know who did it and haven't told the cops. Yet.

I couldn't sleep last night. Images of Lester slumped behind the dumpster haunted me. I avoided Dad when I got home from the church, worried he'd read the secret on my face. I tried to do my homework, but couldn't concentrate. Words on the pages blurred together into nothing.

And now here I am with McGeezer's lumpy nose an inch from my face. "Mr. Kaminsky?" he demands. "What do you think?"

I know *about what?* is the wrong thing to say. "Yes, sir," I mumble.

He grunts and stalks away. A guy behind me snickers. "You have balls, dude," he whispers.

My mind drifts off during class, but Mr. McGeezer keeps calling on me, trying to make me an example. Some of the answers I get right, but a lot I don't. He raises an eyebrow and looks at the rest of the class, as if it's to be expected I'll screw up. It makes me mad. By the end of class, I want to toss my chair at the guy.

"Mr. Kaminsky," he calls as we pack up. I grit my teeth and turn to him. "Come here." He waves a pink slip of paper in front of me. "This is your detention slip. The teacher in charge will sign it and you will return it to me tomorrow."

I take it from him. His fingers are short and stubby. Students for his next class trickle in. "You're off to a rough start."

I don't need him to tell me that.

LINCOLN

"You gotta earn your keep," Rat says. I know it's more than that. Henry wants me busy. Doesn't want me thinking about Lester, or what happened to him in the alley. What we did to him in the alley.

Everything in Al's garage is covered in black grease. Even Rat. "You're like my errand boy." He smirks at me, and I think he's never had anyone to boss around before and this is going to be the shittiest job ever.

"You know anything about cars, besides how to steal them?" he asks. We're standing over an engine. Smell of oil thick in my nose. On the other side of the building is the chop shop, but there's nothing to connect the two businesses except a small door. The engine I'm looking at is here for a legit repair.

I shake my head.

"You good at puzzles? Cuz that's what it's like. Same puzzle over and over. The pieces all fit together and they gotta go back the same way they came out."

He lets the hood slam down and I jump, even though I knew it was coming.

"But for now, you're just gonna do some cleaning." He points to a bucket covered in oily smudges. A cloth, so grimy I can't tell what colour it used to be, hangs over the edge. "Start with the john."

I want to tell him to screw off and kick the bucket across the room. But Henry told me to do whatever Rat said. If I want to stay at the clubhouse, there are rules. I bottle it up so he won't see how pissed off I am.

Magazine pictures of naked girls are taped to the walls. I keep looking at them while I scrub the floor, sink, and toilet. Their big tits filled like helium balloons, skin too tanned.

I poured so much lemon cleaner into the bucket, it blocks out the stink of the room. A stripe of rust from the leaky tap has stained the sink, but I don't bother scrubbing it cuz I'll never get it out. The mirror is chipped and dotted with splotches of brown where the backing's peeled off. I catch my reflection and stop scrubbing for a second.

I don't want to be cleaning up someone else's piss and shit. I want to be at school with Koob, me and him hanging out on a bench planning our next piece, or at his apartment doing homework while his dad cooks something that smells like frying onions but tastes good.

Rat knocks on the door. "You done yet?"

"Almost," I call and swish the toilet brush around the bowl, scrubbing so hard, I think it will snap.

Snap like Lester's bones. I try not to think about it, but it pops into my head anyway. The feel of the tire iron in my hands, how each swing marked his body. And then Henry's boot splitting his head.

Vomit rises in my mouth. I swallow it back, but my stomach heaves again.

All the cleaning wasted as chunks of barf splatter the sides of the toilet bowl.

JAKUB

I do my detention and get off the bus before my stop. I've been cooped up all day. Walking halfway home gives me a chance to think about things. By the time I turn onto my street, my feet are sore and my back hurts from lugging ten pounds of books. My blazer probably smells like B.O.

Dad will know about Lester by now. Laureen, too. I trudge up the stairs like my backpack is full of bricks.

I put my ear to the door of the apartment and listen for a minute. It's quiet. I put my key in the lock and open the door. Dinner's not ready. Hasn't even been started and it's almost seven o'clock. I look at Dad. He's on the couch and stands up slowly. His eyes are puffy and his nose glows red. He lets me dump my backpack on the floor before coming to me with outstretched arms. "Sit down," he says. I throw him a worried look, like I have no idea what he's going to tell me, and pull out a kitchen chair. He sits opposite me.

"Lester," he begins and his eyebrows draw together. Saying his name is painful. My chest aches watching him. I wish I could save him the agony and blurt out that I already know.

"Yesterday. Found in an alley, beaten. Like a dog. Bastards." The words burrow into me, digging into a deep place to fester.

"W-who did it?" I stutter, exhausted from the walk and everything else.

Dad shakes his head. "Don't know." His face twists against the tears threatening to fall. "The police are here. They want to talk to everyone."

My breath comes out shaky and I hold my head in my hands, pressing them against my skull to make the pounding stop. "Everyone?" I repeat.

"They want to know if he was in trouble with anyone, if he had any enemies. I already told them Lester had no enemies. He was a good man."

I shake my head. I don't trust myself to hold it together. A cop, Dad, anyone will see the truth on my face. If they ask if anyone had a grudge against Lester? My mouth will say no, but my brain, my body, will scream *YES*. Did anyone want to hurt Lester? *YES*.

Was he involved with gangs?

YES.

There's a knock at the door. "That's probably the police," he says. "I told them to come back."

The cops. I grab Dad's sleeve. "I can't talk to them right now," I whisper.

He looks at me, confused. "But they need to talk to you!"

"No." I shake my head. "I can't. Tomorrow, maybe."

His face sags. He's too tired to argue.

A voice calls from the hallway. "Mr. Kaminsky? It's Detective Evans."

"Coming!" Dad shuffles to the door. I move to a corner of the couch, hidden from view.

"Sorry to bother you again. I wondered if your son was home yet? Thought I could ask him some questions, so I don't have to come back tomorrow."

"Yes, he's home, but he's not doing well. The news about Lester came as a shock."

"Of course. They were close? Your son and Lester?"

"Yes." I imagine the cop scribbling that down in his notebook.

"You have my card. Call me when your son feels up to talking. How old did you say he was?"

"Fifteen."

"I'm sorry, again, for your loss."

Dad mumbles thanks and shuts the door. I expect him to grill me about why I don't want to speak to the cops, but he doesn't. He sits down beside me on the couch and lays a hand on my knee. "It's okay, Jakub. You'll talk when you're ready."

I nod, but the room turns blurry as everything I've kept wrapped tight unwinds.

LINCOLN

Henry's on the front porch, talking with Butch. They both have smokes in their hands. Henry takes an angry draw on his and blows the smoke out in a hard puff.

The way Butch looks at me makes me stare at my shoes and hurry past him into the house. "There's your answer, right there," he says to Henry, and he means me, but I don't know why.

Inside it's quiet. The front window is open so I can hear Henry and Butch talking. Butch was in prison, too; he and Henry shared a cell for a while and hatched a plan about getting the Red Bloodz running again. Started with the chop shop, but I know it doesn't end there.

"That's where the quick money is. Get a few kids like him on the streets and we've got cash flow. Feed it through the shop and it's buried. Cops have to look real hard to find it. I'm telling you, get that kid selling for us at Wilson, maybe a couple other schools. Recruit more young ones. Give them a taste of the life."

Henry takes a deep breath. "I don't know, man," he says with an exhale. "I want to fly low. Dealing gets us noticed. I got eighteen months left on my parole."

"Gets us money." He drops his voice low. "You're not dealing, the kid is. How old is he? Fourteen? Fifteen? He's still a juvie. Same as with the cars. He'll barely do time if he gets caught. Record gets wiped at eighteen."

"I'll think about it."

"Think fast. I'm around till Wednesday and then I'm taking off."

Butch's heavy footsteps on the wooden porch rattle the glass as he leaves. I jump away from the window and go to the kitchen. The shelves are bare. "Nothing to eat," I mutter, slamming a cupboard door shut.

"You hungry?" Henry asks. I didn't hear him come inside. He flicks his butt into the sink. A trail of smoke twists to the ceiling.

"What's Butch want?"

He narrows his eyes. "I asked if you were hungry."

I glower at him. "I spent the day wiping piss off toilets and taking orders from Rat. Hell yeah, I'm hungry."

With a snort of laughter, he calls to two guys playing vids in the other room. "I'm taking my little brother out. You two shits stay here." He waits a second, but neither of them say anything, so he stomps into the living room. I hear a controller clatter down and the couch scrape on the floor. "You hear me?"

"Shit!" one guy yells. "Yeah! I heard you." He's mad, but too scared of Henry to do anything. I can hear it in his voice.

"Come on," he barks at me. His face is all twisted up, like how Mom gets when the landlord won't fix something at our house.

I follow, cuz what else can I do?

As I walk behind him to a car, one with new plates and paint, I know that if my brother asks me to deal for him, I'll have to. I don't have a choice.

I think about Dustin and how he's still with Mom and Dad. I left to save him, but it's all backfiring. I'm getting sucked in so deep, I'll never get out.

I won't do this to Dustin, I swear. I'd rather never see him again than pull him under with me.

I can't sleep. It's not just because the clubhouse throbs all night. It's cuz I see Lester in the shadows and hear him moaning for me to help him.

I toss and turn for a while, then get my shoes on. I need to clear my head. There's people on the porch, sitting in a cloud of pot smoke. Roxy's one of them. She doesn't see me, so I keep walking, get to the end of the sidewalk, and figure I may as well keep walking some more. My hand slides into my jacket pocket, wraps around a switchblade I found in a kitchen drawer.

I like knowing it's there. I run my finger around the smooth curved edge. I imagine I'm a ninja warrior, whipping out the blade, flipping and jumping around my attacker, the knife spinning in the air. I think of how, in my old life, me and Koob had our secret identities. Morf and Skar. We were kind of like ninjas sneaking around in the night, only we were writing, not fighting.

I stop myself from thinking about it. I have to squash those memories. And forget about being a ninja. I know that if anyone came after me, it would be clumsy. Two people tousling and grunting till one accidentally staggers back with a groan. How it was with Lester. Heavy breathing, sweat, and then a slow-spreading red splotch. No ninja moves. Just ugly.

With my shoulders hunched and my head tucked under my hood, I disappear in the shadows. I'm halfway to nowhere when my feet move in a different direction. Toward the alley behind Fenty's. There's still police tape up, blocking off the area. I don't want to, but I start remembering the sound of the tire iron hitting his body. The sickening thud. How he didn't run, just lay there, like he knew he didn't stand a chance. I relive every hit with the tire iron till heat prickles on my neck and I think I'll puke.

But it was Henry who took the final swings. Lester was still breathing when I stepped away. It was Henry's boot that cracked his skull. I might have hurt him, but Henry killed him.

I leave the alley and walk around to the front of the bar. The weather's changing. Tonight, the air is sharp and cold. I'm glad I have my jacket. A few guys stumble out of Fenty's. I watch them. They light a cigarette and share a laugh about something.

I guess I'm staring at them, because one calls to me. "You want something?" I shouldn't keep hanging around like this. They're both watching me, waiting for me to leave.

"Got a smoke?" I ask, walking closer to them. The light above the door makes their faces glow yellow. One guy is wearing an apron under his jacket. It hangs down past his knees and has brown grease stains on it.

They look at me and snicker. I hear one make a crack about my age. Baby-smooth skin on the side of my face, and a scrawny neck, make me look younger than I am.

His friend gives me a pissed-off look and takes his pack of smokes out. It's halfway empty. He pulls one out and stretches his arm to give it to me. I reach out with my left hand, and real quick, pull the knife out of my hoodie pocket. It clicks into place and glints in the light. They both back up, but I've got the guy's wrist. I'm squeezing it tight.

They look at me like they're not so sure. Like maybe they *could* jump me and get the knife, or maybe not. Depends how desperate I am, that's what they're thinking. And they don't know.

"Take the smokes. Is that what you want?"

There's a roar in my ears, and I can't believe the knife in my hand is pointed at them.

The guy in the apron tosses his butt on the ground and holds up his hands. "My break's over, okay? We got to go back inside. My boss'll be coming to check on me."

My chest heaves. I hold the knife tighter and move the tip closer to the guy's face. I want him to see that it's real. He angles his face away, so all I see is his chin.

He's afraid. One vein bulges in his neck. "I could cut you," I whisper.

"No, no, don't. We're just on our break. That's it. We gotta go back in now."

Fenty's door opens, and all of a sudden music fills the alley. I don't look to see who opened the door, but I let go of the guy's hand and start running. Down the street and around a corner. I fold up the knife and hold it in my hand. After a few blocks, I stop running. But I hold the knife tightly, the metal warm, like a hot stone, in my palm.

My breath comes out in foggy puffs, but I'm not cold anymore. The run warmed me up. I go past a tattoo place. Henry knows the guys that run it. They come by the clubhouse sometimes, ink the new Red Bloodz. It's still open; the windows are bright with light and two guys sit at the desk. One has his feet up, the other's staring at his phone. There's a whole chart of different designs in the window. A dagger, like Henry's, is in the middle.

"Hey," I say, walking in. The door makes a beeping noise. It smells like ink and rubbing alcohol and stings my nose. They both turn and look at me. The guy puts his feet on the floor.

"Help you?" he asks. His arms are covered with sleeves of colour.

I take some twenties out of my pocket and put them on the counter. "Can you do one for me?"

He looks me up and down, like he's going to send me away. "I'm Henry's brother." I blurt quick. "He sent me."

"Oh, yeah." He still looks unsure. "How old are you?"

"Eighteen," I lie, my eyes shifty.

He snorts cuz he knows it's bullshit. "Got any ID?"

"Lost it."

He looks to his buddy, who shrugs. *What do they care?* I wonder. *I've got the cash.* He takes the money off the counter and stuffs it in his pocket. "What do you want?"

"A dagger," I say.

"Can't do the Red Bloodz one, you know that, right?"

"Yeah," I say. "I want one like it."

He shakes his head. "Sorry, man."

"How about this?" I grab a piece of paper and a pencil and draw a dagger stabbing through a grinning skull, a few drops of black blood drip down.

"That's pretty good," he mumbles.

"Gimme a few minutes." He goes to a desk with a light above it and draws out the tracer. He asks where I want it and how big.

I take off my jacket and hang it on a hook and sit in the chair at his station. The vinyl is slippery and cold. With only a T-shirt, my skin prickles with goosebumps.

He holds a thin piece of paper in his hands and nods at the chair by his tools. He slaps the paper on, rubs the ink onto my skin, and peels it off. A minute later, the buzz of the needle hits my arm. I clench my teeth when it bites into my skin.

I don't say anything. I close my eyes and listen to the hum of the needle as it marks me.

When he's done, I sit up. My arm is sore. It aches and stings at the same time. "Go take a look," he says. So I do. I hold my arm sideways in the mirror.

"What do you think?" he asks, peeling off the gloves.

I stare at the too bright colours and the puffy redness. "Colours will fade a bit," he tells me. I nod, but don't say anything else cuz I'm trying to figure out who I got it for. Me? Henry? Lester? Or Koob?

The door jingles and someone walks in. I know who it is and duck my head. "Where'd the poster go?" she says. The guy at the desk looks up and shrugs. She takes a deep, angry breath, but doesn't say anything. She pulls a poster out of her bag and tapes it onto the door.

She marches over to me, even though I'm not looking at her. "Have you seen this girl?" She holds up a poster of Missing Rachelle. The one with long hair.

I don't say anything, but she shoves the paper closer to my face. "Can you look at the picture?" She sounds desperate. There's dark circles under her eyes.

"Never seen her."

The girl takes a deep breath and sighs. "Of course you haven't," she mutters. Then she stuffs the posters into her backpack and zips it shut. "No one sees anything in this goddamn city." She slams the door hard when she leaves and the mirrors on the wall rattle.

The guy who did my tattoo tapes a layer of plastic on top of it, and I slide my jacket back on. Now what? I think. Back to the clubhouse? And my stomach sinks cuz where else is there?

Roxy/Rachelle's sister is still outside, talking to some girls on the corner. "Have you seen her?" she asks.

"Gawd, leave us alone. Go ask that guy," one of them says, turning away from her. She comes toward me, but her steps slow when she realizes she already did.

"Let me see that picture again," I say. We're standing under a streetlight and I hold the photo up, squinting at it. "I think I did see her a few days ago. At a house party."

"Oh my god," she gasps. "Where? Do you know the address? Was she with anyone?" Roxy's sister is so relieved, she's almost crying. "Was she okay?"

"Yeah, she was fine." I'm scrambling for a lie. "I don't remember the house, though. It was somewhere around here, in the West End."

She takes a card out of her backpack. Her hand trembles when she hands it to me. Roxy's photo is on the front. A cell number and her sister's name, Charlene, is on the back. "Call me if you see her again, okay? Can you at least do that, so I know she's okay?"

I nod and take the card with my left hand cuz my other arm hurts too much. "I gotta go," I tell her. I feel her eyes on me till I turn the corner. *Why'd I say anything?* I wonder, and I feel like an asshole. I got her hopes up for nothing. Rachelle's not missing; she's just missing to her sister. I know exactly where she is.

JAKUB

After school the next day, I hear Father Dom's beat-up mini van through the open window as it chokes and whines its way down the block. Dad and I are in the apartment. I'm doing homework, but Dad sits silently on the couch. Not much to say since he found out about Lester.

A few minutes later, Father Dom knocks on the door. Dad rises halfway out of his seat, but I'm already up and heading for the door. He'll be here under the guise of checking on us, to see how we're handling the news about Lester. But I know that's not the real reason. He wants to know why I haven't gone to the cops.

"We need to talk," Father Dom insists quietly when I open the door. His face is flushed and he glares at me. My stomach drops. "Antony!" he calls inside. "I need Jakub's help at church. We had some books delivered and we have to move them. Can I take him with me?"

Dad stands up, limps to the door, and looks at me. "Yes, of course," he says.

Father Dom shoots me a sideways look.

"We won't be long," he assures Dad. I slip my shoes on and follow Father Dom down the stairs. He's got a sweatshirt on with black pants, his white collar peeking out at his neck. He mutters prayers for forgiveness for his lie. We both know there are no books to move.

It's not until we're inside the van that Father Dom turns to me. "Have you gone to the police yet?"

I fumble for an excuse, but nothing comes. He gives an impatient sigh.

A pounding starts in my forehead.

"What are you waiting for?"

"The cops might put it together without me saying anything," I mutter.

"This is not how your father raised you!"

His words are like a kick in the balls. I don't want to think about what Dad would do if he found out I knew who'd killed Lester and hadn't said anything. I slouch lower in my seat and stare outside. The curtains flutter in the window of our apartment. Dad's watching from above, waiting for us to leave.

Father Dom turns the key in the ignition. It makes a grinding noise, and the van jumps when he puts it into gear. "Piece of shit," he mutters. I don't know if he's talking about the van, or me.

"We can't keep this a secret, Jakub."

"We?" I say, nervous. "I thought you couldn't tell anyone. What about your vows?"

Father Dom swerves around a corner and into the other lane. He gets a long, angry honk. "Antony needs to know. You are his son. He can help you in ways I can't."

"But he'll call the cops!"

He grips the steering wheel. "I know."

My face burns with frustration. "The cops will go after Lincoln. And the Red Bloodz." I bite down on my lip to stop the wave of panic that washes over me.

"Good." Father Dom's voice is cold.

I let out a shaky exhalation. Things were getting so tangled: pulling one string loose would knot something else. Telling the cops about Lincoln and the Red Bloodz would lead them to the chop shop and the stolen cars. It wasn't a far leap for the cops to put Lincoln together with the carjacking at St. Bart's. They had his prints and the cellphone photos. How long till they figure out I'm the connection? My future is on the line now. Me and Link, forever tied together. If he goes down, I'll be right behind, the weight of him like an anchor.

Father Dom parks the van in the alley behind the church. He sits for a minute after turning off the ignition. "Is there more?" he asks.

I swallow, because now is the time to tell him everything. Instead of shaking my head, I nod. My conscience can only take so much. I'm going to crack under the weight. Better to admit it all to Father Dom and have his help than let it fester in me.

He sighs and purses his lips. "Tell me."

I want to go inside, to the cool of the church where I can stay hidden in the dark of the confessional, but Father Dom doesn't make a move to get out of the van.

A pounding starts in my forehead. "It was Link's idea, I mean, most of it. He was only going to take one."

"One what?" Father Dom asks.

"A car ... from St. Bart's."

"Oh, shit," Father Dom swears under his breath. "The one with the girl in it?"

"That was after. He came back a second time. I told him not to, but he didn't listen. He didn't know there was a kid inside the Escalade. You know Link, he wouldn't —"

"Hurt someone?" Father Dom asks, pointedly.

"He just needed a getaway."

Father Dom sits shaking his head in disbelief. "I don't know what to say to you, Jakub. This is not who you are!"

A wave of guilt washes over me. It hits like a typhoon, knocking me over, making me scramble to hold on to something solid. "I was trying to help Lincoln. I owed him. I thought it was just going to be one car." I fumble for excuses, but they only enrage Father Dom.

"Owed him for what?"

Was it just the night he got picked up by the cops? Maybe I've always been trying to pay him back, apologizing for the differences between us.

When I don't answer, Father Dom says, "The graffiti, I looked past. Maybe I shouldn't have. It led you down this road." His face contorts with regret. His eyebrows furrow and he frowns. "But this! Jakub, stealing a car, concealing a murder! Who are you?"

Father Dom's voice rings in my ears. Who am I?

"I don't know," I say and start to cry. It starts as a low whimper, but gets louder till my shoulders are shaking and I'm howling.

My stomach's in knots, but I know I have to tell Lincoln tonight, before I chicken out. Father Dom took my confession, properly. And this is my penance. My way to make it right. I have to tell Dad and, on Monday, go into Father O'Shea's office and tell him everything. Father Dom helped me write it out, so I wouldn't forget anything. Makes it easier to say if I can read it.

He asked me who I am. Am I the kid who steals cars and covers up murders? I'm not. Inside, I know I'm not. But that's who I've turned into.

I rap on Lincoln's door and look around. Same broken toys and shit all over the front yard. Through the front window, I can see the couch still sagging in the middle because of a busted leg.

Dustin answers, wearing the bottoms of superhero pajamas. "What happened to your face?" he asks.

"Got jumped," I tell him. He eyes my fading bruises, but his expression doesn't change.

"Link's not here," he says.

"Who is it?" his mom calls from inside.

"Koob," he shouts to her.

I hear a snort from inside the house, and then she

comes to the door and shoos Dustin away. "He packed a bag and left."

"Where'd he go?" I ask, even though I know the answer.

She shrugs and I almost turn to go because she doesn't answer for so long. "Heard he was working at the garage on Mountain." She gives me a look and I see the regret on her face. "If you find him, tell him his little brother's asking for him."

I nod and walk back down to the sidewalk. The screen door slaps shut behind me and I see Dustin at the window, his belly pressing against the glass as he watches me walk away.

Gravel crunches under my feet as I walk up the main drive. A sign with "Al's Automotive Repair" in faded blue letters hangs across the front of the building. The yard is surrounded by a chain-link fence. The garage's overhead door is open, and a gritty mess of tools and supplies fills the place. One car sits on a hoist, and outside, two beaters on blocks fill one side of the lot. Nothing to prove it's a chop shop, but if I go around the back, I bet it's a different story.

I wait in the empty yard for a long time. Too nervous to ring the bell or shout for attention. There's security cameras, but after years of painting, I've gotten good at avoiding them. Finally, the side door opens. I duck in case it's one of the other guys. But it's not. Link dumps a bucket of water on the ground. He's going to go back inside unless I call out to him.

"Link!"

He looks around, his eyes covered with his hat, a new one. Sitting stiff on his head. When he spots me, he gives a quick check inside the garage, drops the bucket beside the door, and walks over.

"What are you doing here?" he asks, pushing back the brim of his hat. He blinks, his nervous twitch in overdrive.

"I need to talk."

"*Here?* What the hell?" He walks over quick and shoves me back to the road, glancing over his shoulder. "I'll get in shit if anyone sees you here."

I shift uncomfortably. I pull his hat out of the pocket of my hoodie and hold it out to him. He takes it and stuffs it into his back pocket. There's so much I have to say, but none of it makes any sense with him in front of me. I have to start somewhere, though. "There's been cops at the apartment asking questions."

His voice catches. "What did you —"

"Nothing. I didn't talk to them."

Link rubs a hand over his face, pushing off his hat to wipe his brow. "Everything's so fucked up." There are dark circles under his eyes. He gives a long exhale, blowing out a breath that hasn't seen a toothbrush in days.

"You could tell the cops," I say quietly. "Stop protecting him."

Lincoln stares at the ground, kicking at gravel. He doesn't say anything. *It would save me from ratting you out.*

"Link?"

He opens his mouth to say something, then closes it and shakes his head. "I'm not a snitch." He shoots another worried look at the garage and grabs my sleeve, pulling me farther away.

I look at my friend. Below the sleeve of his T-shirt, a tattoo, newly inked. "When did you get that?" I ask, pointing at it.

"Yesterday." His eyes stray to the tattoo, like he's just remembered he has it. "You better go." Resignation makes his voice flat. "Rat's in the back. He might come out for a smoke."

"Link, there's something else." A clatter of tools inside the garage makes Link jump.

"What?" he asks, his voice tight with irritation.

I stand there, clinging to what I need to tell him. The stupid, ridiculous idea that it will matter. That it will change things.

The tattoo, what he's already done for the gang, what he's going to have to do; they've got him. He's not getting out now. I don't have to worry about my confession hurting Lincoln. The Lincoln I want to protect is gone.

"It's a message from Dustin. He misses you," I tell him, my voice tight.

A flicker of the old Link crosses his face, then disappears.

He shakes his head at me, his eyes distant. "Just fucking *go*," he says.

He heads back to the garage, head bent low, shoulders slumped. I watch him cross the street and then I turn away, too. There's a gaping hole where he used to be, like someone ripped out a piece of me and forgot to stitch it up.

The city stretches below me. A breeze makes goose-bumps rise on my arms. I pull the bandana up over my nose and mouth and get to work.

I sketched quickly when I left the garage, emotion making the lines raw and powerful. On the roof of the building, the wind flips the pages of my sketchbook, threatening to carry it over the edge.

Using my backpack to anchor it open, I study the piece. There's no mistaking what it means. A guy staring out at the world, his mouth gagged by a Red Bloodz tag. The dagger from the tattoo stabbing him in the back.

I hold a can of red spray paint in my hand. With a hiss, Morf hits the wall.

I won't rat on Henry, but I can't stay silent, either. Hidden in the pages of my sketchbook are drawings of Lester, the truth of his murder. They need to make their way onto a wall so Morf can speak for the dead, lay blame where it needs to be.

LINCOLN

I hear people partying at the clubhouse from down the street. Bursts of laughter sound like crows cawing. I want to be anywhere else but here. But there is nowhere else. I brush past four or five people on the porch to get to the door.

Inside, the air is thick with smoke. "Linnnncoooooln," someone yells. I turn and it's Roxy. Her legs hang over the arm of a chair. There's a lamp behind her, but the shade is gone, so it shines too bright and I squint when I look at her.

"Where've you been?" I ask, coming closer. She's drunk, or high, or both. Her mouth turns up in a smile and her half-closed eyes are glassy.

"Around." She sits up in the chair like she just had an idea. "Hey, I'm thinking about hitching west, to Vancouver. I don't want to be hanging around here in the winter. Frickin' freezing."

I don't know if she's being serious or not. I blink at her a couple times, waiting. "When are you leaving?"

She shrugs. "Soon, I guess."

I think about her sister searching the city for someone who's long gone. "You gonna tell anyone before you go?"

"I'm telling you," she slurs.

I tiptoe around the words, worried I'll say too much. "What about your sister?"

Roxy tugs at a loose thread on the chair, wrapping it around her finger till the tip turns blue. "She'll just make me go home."

"What's wrong with that?"

"Cuz, I can't go back." She sits back in the chair with a huff. "I got messed up in some stuff. I needed to get away. You know how it is."

"You needed some air." I'm fighting for breath right now, I want to tell her. When Koob came by the shop, I thought about leaving with him. Walking away like all this shit with the Red Bloodz never happened. My insides screamed at me to do it. But my feet, my head, they went the other way, back to the garage.

"Yeah," she says and looks around. "But now I need more air. This place is getting to me."

"You feel like you're suffocating," I mumble, cuz it's all familiar.

Her breath catches in her throat in a little hiccup and she nods. "I knew you'd get it."

"You want company?" I ask, half joking.

"Yeah. You'd come?" she asks.

I let the idea float for a few minutes, thinking. "Why not?" I think about Dustin. Maybe it'd be better for him if I was gone. "You know anyone we could stay with?" I ask.

Roxy's eyelids are heavy, like she might pass out soon. "Where?" She tries to focus on me, but can't.

"Vancouver."

"Oh." She tries to sit up, but flops back down, her forehead wrinkling cuz she's confused. "You're going to Van? That's cool." I look at her and shake my head. There's no point talking to her when she's like this.

Vancouver. The idea makes me light-headed. People leave their home all the time. Lester was going to. Roxy did it, she ended up here, but still, she had the balls to leave. We'd be free. Me and Roxy, heading west.

I leave Roxy on the chair and go upstairs. I don't want to party. I just want quiet. A couple of guys jostle me on the stairs, but I ignore them. When I get to my room — and it's only my room cuz no one else is in it and my duffle bag's sitting in the corner — I lock the door, flop on the mattress, and stare at the glowing light bulb until I see spots. The word *Vancouver* runs through my head over and over until it turns into a nothing word and just a feeling: an escape.

There's a cannon tucked into my hoodie pocket. I take it out and stop in front of a random grey door. Paint hits the metal and a few drops roll down. Henry told me to tag the shit out of the West End. People need to know we're here; we need to make a mark.

I'm better than this. I didn't tell him that, but tagging

is old. I know what Koob and I can do together. There's no thrill in tossing up a gang tag, no art either.

A mailbox gets one, and a garage door and a loading dock. A dumpster in a back alley already has others, but I make the Red Bloodz tag bigger, so it takes up the whole side. A fire escape stretches up above the dumpster. I look around, pulling back my hoodie to check, and sure enough, I'm in the alley where I got busted. I saved Koob that night. He was shitting his pants thinking about what would happen if the cops brought him home. What Mr. K would do.

I never go up buildings by myself. Too scared. I only go up because Koob does. I look at the fire escape, the way it zigzags up the building. I know what's up there. Before I let my fear stop me, I climb onto the dumpster, the lid bending and creaking under my feet. Then, my hands are on the fire escape railing, rust flaking off, marking me black with sooty dust. The metal clanks under my feet, loose bolts making it shake as I go to the top.

The wind is stronger on the roof, the air more biting. Gravel crunches under my feet and I walk around, close to the edge. I hate the edge, but I dare myself to look over. To take a breath. I close my eyes, imagining for a second what would happen if I fell. The splat I'd make. Like Lester, a mass of broken bones and exploded insides. It makes me dizzy thinking about it and I step back, gasping.

I turn to the wall. Koob's piece, the one we worked on, is still there. A can of spray paint crushes the city.

Our tags in red at the bottom. Morf. Skar.

I stare at it for a few minutes, trying to remember who I was the night we painted it.

I toss the cannon at the wall as hard as I can, but it just rebounds off and falls to the ground at my feet. I want to tear the piece apart, brick by brick, so there's nothing left to remind me of what we used to be.

JAKUB

I open the front door. Same smells of mildew and wet wood in the hallway. Worn carpet and pulsing fluorescent bulbs lead the way upstairs.

Dad's cooking; the thick aroma of borscht fills the hallway. Salami, too, the garlic released by the heat of the frying pan.

The door gives a familiar creak as it opens. Father Dom is here, sitting at the kitchen table. He waves a hand in greeting, his face heavy with what he knows. With what he knows I still have to do.

I reach into the hot pan for a piece of the salami. Dad slaps at my hand, but I take one quick and blow on it till it cools enough to eat it. There's four bowls on the counter. Dad fills them with thick, creamy borscht. He adds a dollop of sour cream and swirls it into the soup. "What's going on?" I ask, looking between them.

"It's for Lester." He shrugs. "I wanted to do something. Laureen's coming, too. I'll go tell her it's ready."

As he bends down to slip on his shoes, I hear him groan and lean against the wall, clutching his thigh.

"Dad?"

"Antony?" Father Dom says, rising from his chair. He waves us off.

"It's nothing. A twinge, that's all." But I see his face, forehead wrinkled and mouth screwed up as he tries to hide the pain.

"I'll go get Laureen," I say.

"No." He turns to me, his eyes resolute. I open my mouth to argue, but his Polish pride flares. "I'm fine."

"Fine," I mutter as the door clicks shut behind him. Hearing his uneven footsteps in the hallway makes me shake my head at Father Dom. He reaches into the inside pocket of his jacket and slides it across the table at me.

"Look." He jabs a finger at it.

I lean over. It's a clipping from today's paper; the bolded headline reads: "Suspect Arrested in Fenty's Bar Killing." I grip the table and sit down. "They caught Henry?" I exhale.

But Father Dom shakes his head. "Read it."

Police have arrested 32-year-old Lawrence Girard for the murder of 53-year-old Lester McFarlane. McFarlane's body was found badly beaten in an alley behind Fenty's Bar, in the West End, on Oct. 3. Girard was arrested for on unrelated charge later that night and police found McFarlane's wallet

in his possession. Police suspect robbery
led to McFarlane's beating and subsequent
death.

Father Dom drops his voice to a rushed whisper.
"I know him." He taps the photos. "He comes to the
soup kitchen, brings his children." He grabs my hand,
squeezing it hard. "This can't go on. You have to tell
the police."

The room feels like it's shrinking, the walls swirling
around me. "You don't get it!" I blurt out, frustration
straining my voice. "You think if they arrest Henry, this
will be over? His crew will come after me. And Dad.
They'll turn on Lincoln, if they think he snitched."

I take the article off the table, fold it, and stuff it
in my back pocket. My heart's still beating quick when
Dad and Laureen shuffle through the door. She's wearing her slippers and the ends of her hair are curled tight
and springy. Dad goes to the counter and brings back
a half-empty bottle of vodka, another gift from Father
Dom. He pours a mouthful into each of our water
glasses, even mine.

"To Lester," he says.

"To Lester," we chorus. The liquid goes down my
throat, settling in my stomach like hot charcoal.

"Feels empty around here," Laureen says. The first
spoonful of borscht sits on her spoon. "He was a good
guy, you know. Always paid his rent on time. Never
gave me any trouble. Not like —" She points to the

apartment downstairs with a raised eyebrow. Mr. and Mrs. Domestic Abuse. "Heard they caught somebody." She looks to us for confirmation.

Father Dom nods. "It was in the paper this morning."

"Goddamn son of a bitch," Laureen swears and looks quickly at Father Dom. "No offence," she says.

He waves her apology away.

"I hope he gets sent away for life." Her face twists with bitterness.

"Me too," Dad mutters.

I sit between them, the truth smouldering inside me.

A car, a low-rider, drives past, slowly. Its suspension creaks as it goes over a pothole. I bend my shoulders under my hoodie, sticking to the shadows. I snuck out when Dad's snores filled the apartment, raiding the garage for what was left of my cannons.

It's closing time for Fenty's Bar. People stumble on the sidewalk, leaning against each other; fragments of conversations float past me, most of them slurred. I duck into the alley, where I found Lester. The yellow police tape is gone, and I say a prayer when I pass the spot where he lay. It's too dark to see, but I imagine his blood still stains the pavement.

I jump onto one of the dumpsters and cling to windowsills a couple of inches thick until I can get to the fire escape and climb up to the roof. Only it's not me three storeys above the alley, it's Morf. Daring, bold Morf going places Jakub would never venture. The payoff is big. A piece in this location could run for weeks, maybe months, too tricky to buff. That's what this piece deserves.

Morf will speak for me. His voice will scream loud; it will echo off the cement walls until everyone hears.

I put on my bandana, feel the familiar clunk of the ball against the sides of the cannon. My sketchbook lies open at my feet. I don't need it, though; the image I'm painting tonight was burned into my memory days ago.

When the final hiss of the spray can hits the stucco wall, I take a step back and look at Lester lying in the alley, a work boot off to the side. His face half-covered by hair. "RIP Lester" scrawled in bubble letters under him.

The Red Bloodz tag hangs ominous over his body.

Tossing the cannons into my backpack, I begin the dangerous climb down. When my feet hit the ground, I look up at the piece. Lester floats above me, and my pulse races. More than anything I've done, this one matters. And there's no mistaking what it means.

LINCOLN

I stand outside my house for a while, watching Dustin through the window. Dad's home with him, sleeping in a chair while Dustin stares at the TV. With my hood up, I'm invisible in the shadows. I wait until Dustin falls asleep, too, stretched out on the couch, one arm dangling to the floor.

I think about sneaking inside, lying down in my own bed. More than anything, I want to press rewind. I want back into my house, into the life I had. But it doesn't work that way. I'm not that guy anymore. I'm on the outside now and there's no getting back in.

Knowing what I gave up makes my chest hurt, like a hole is burning through my ribs. I turn away, slinking back to where I came from.

My phone's been ringing all night. It goes again, making my pocket vibrate. I take it out, pull out the SIM card, and drop it down the sewer grate. I toss the phone onto the road; the plastic cracks and shatters. I can't go back, but I don't have to go on, either. Maybe I can run away with Roxy, leave all the shit behind and start fresh somewhere new.

I'm still carrying around Roxy's sister's card. It's in my pocket. If Roxy hitches out west, her sister will never find her. I wonder about the stuff Roxy got mixed up in, if it's as bad as she thinks it is.

When I get to the clubhouse, Roxy is outside, having a smoke. Her hood is pulled up over her head, sleeves pulled long over her fingers. She's chewed a hole on the cuff part, so her thumb sticks out.

The ring in her eyebrow glints in the dark, catching light from the bare bulb on the porch.

"It's friggin' cold out," she says when I get close. I point to the flip-flops on her feet. No shit, she's cold.

"You could smoke inside."

She shakes her head. "I needed some air."

I get a weird twinge. "How come?"

She takes a long drag and blows the smoke out the other side of her mouth. "Doesn't matter. You got any weed?"

"Not on me. Probably some inside, though."

She's staring across the street, shivering. My feet tap the stairs. Spongy, rotten boards hide the sound.

"Saw my sister today."

I turn to her quick, surprised.

"She didn't see me, though. She was asking about me, to anyone who passed by. She was always like that, pushy."

"Did you talk to her?"

Roxy shakes her head and her shoulders slump. "I wanted to, but there's so much —" Roxy breaks off. "She'll hate me."

I take the smoke from her and take a long puff. "You think she'd still be looking for you if she did?"

Roxy's quiet and I hope she's thinking about it. I pass the cigarette back to her and she takes a drag off it, blowing a stream of smoke into the night.

My hands go to my pocket, brush against the softened edges of the Missing Rachelle card. "Were you serious about going out to Vancouver?" I ask.

She takes so long to answer, I wonder if she heard me. "I don't know."

"If you do, I'm not going," I tell her.

She looks at me, flicking the fringe of hair out of her eyes. "Figured. With your brother and shit."

I snort and shake my head. I want to tell her that just cuz we share blood, doesn't make us brothers.

"They were looking for you before. Henry and the other one," she says. "Asked if I knew where you were."

"You know why?"

She shakes her head. They were probably pissed that I wasn't answering my phone. I pull the card from her sister out of my pocket and hand it to her.

"What is it?" she asks.

"Just look at it," I say. When she does, her mouth goes tight.

There's a pounding of feet through the house and Jonny bursts through the doors. "He's out here!" he hollers into the house.

Roxy looks at me like "I told you" and makes room for me to stand up.

"What?" I say, cuz he's staring at me.

"Why haven't you been answering your fucking phone? Your brother wants to talk to you." The way he says *brother* make me grit my teeth. He's a slimy little shit. He holds the door open, waiting for me, like he's a friggin' bounty hunter. I look at Roxy, but she's staring at the card, the cigarette forgotten in her hand.

I got no choice, I go inside. From the door, I can see Henry at the kitchen table, so I head that way, slowly though, cuz needles of worry move up my spine.

Rat and Butch are sitting at the table, too. Jonny darts to the empty chair and leans back in it. None of them look happy to see me. There aren't any more chairs, so I lean against the counter. It's sticky with spilled beer.

Henry's flipping his phone around in a circle. There's a bottle of Jack Daniel's in front of him, almost empty. No one offers me any.

It's still noisy in the house. One guy walks into the kitchen, takes a look at me and who's around the table, and beats it out of the room. I swallow hard and wish I could leave. I don't know what's going on, but it feels like the day in the car when we drove to the alley to find Lester.

Finally, Henry holds up the phone and shows it to me. I move closer, peering at the screen. A grainy photo, hard to make out. I use my fingers to make it bigger. A graffiti piece, no colour, except for the Red Bloodz tag and one other thing. And I don't have to enlarge the photo to know whose tag I'll see.

A weird thump in my chest makes me go pale. My eyes blink, darting from the phone to the table and back again.

"You know anything about this?"

"No." I give him the phone. But my throat's gone dry and I can't look at him cuz I'm blinking like crazy.

"I only know two graff writers who knew Lester. You and the Polish kid."

"H-how do you know it's Lester?" I stutter.

Henry stands up and holds the back of my neck. He puts the phone right in front of my face. Flecks of spit fly out of his mouth when he shouts at me. "Look at the fucking picture!" I smell the booze on his breath and meet his eyes. They're like a rabid dog's. "You told him, didn't you?" he yells in my face.

I catch a glimpse of Jonny, grinning.

"He guessed." My voice is higher than normal. "Didn't need to tell him."

Henry lets go of me and swears, slamming his hand on the counter.

"We gotta take care of this," Jonny says.

"Like I don't fucking know that?" Henry turns on him. I have a flash of satisfaction watching Jonny's face fall.

"Where's the kid?" Butch asks. His voice is deep and rough like it's been bottled up for too long.

Their eyes are on me again. I get a choking feeling in my throat. What was Koob thinking? He went too far this time. The Red Bloodz can't let a piece like that go unanswered. He's going to pay for it.

"I don't know."

"Find him," Henry says. "Bring him here."

"Why?" I ask. I know it's stupid, but I can't help myself.

"Why the fuck do you think?" Jonny sneers.

Henry comes up real close again, and I lean further back, the counter digging into my spine. "You want in with us. You gotta prove it. Even *I'm* not so sure you know who your real brothers are." He slaps my arm where the tattoo is and I gasp at the jolt of pain. "Go!" he whispers in my face with hot, tangy breath that I have to swallow.

When I get outside, I'm shaking, cuz I don't know what the hell I'm supposed to do. I squeeze the knife in my pocket. They want Koob. Are they gonna beat him? Kill him? Leave him in an alley like Lester? I know I should get moving, find Koob and warn him about what's coming, but my feet won't move. Cuz if I do tell Koob, Henry will come after me, punishment for my faded loyalty.

"Where are you going?"

I didn't notice Roxy. She moved from the steps to the chair on the porch, the same one as the day I met her. In the dark, all I can see is the burning tip of her smoke. "Some shit's going down," I say. "I gotta take care of it."

A truck drives slowly up the street, headlights glowing. It's old, the suspension's gone. Every pothole makes it creak like it's dying. Roxy stands up, hikes a bag up on her shoulder, and comes to stand beside me. She flicks her cigarette onto the grass. "My sister won't let me smoke in the truck."

"Your sister?" I look at her again, the bag she's carrying, and understand. "You called her?"

She doesn't say anything. The truck's front door opens. The shout of "Rachelle" lights up the night like fireworks. Her sister flies across the yard at her, crying and laughing with relief. I watch from the shadows as she holds Roxy's face in her hands. "I'm sorry," Charlene says, gasping and sobbing at the same time. "I never should have —" They hug, and her words are muffled, like whatever it was never mattered anyway.

Roxy's going home. I let the sounds of their reunion, the apologies and explanations follow me as I go into the night. I'm glad one of us is going home. Missing Rachelle got found.

JAKUB

There's nowhere more silent than a church at night. It's still like death.

I wish I could drink it in, let it coat me with quiet. But that's not why I'm here.

Father Dom sits beside me in the pew. He's wearing his black robe, nodding, waiting for me to start talking. I still haven't told Dad. Every time I think about it, my guts start to churn and I feel like I'm gonna puke. And on Monday, I'm supposed to confess everything to Father O'Shea.

"I can't do it." My voice echoes off the stone. A whisper magnified into a shout.

"Jakub!" He takes a breath, reigning in his frustration. "What happens when the police catch Lincoln? Because they will. You two aren't master criminals. The truth will come out and it will be worse for you."

I shake my head, stubbornly. "I'll deal with it then, if it happens. I learned my lesson. I'm done with Lincoln."

"But he hurt people. There are consequences —"

"No!" I shout at him. "I can't do it. I can't give Lincoln to the cops like that. He'd never do that to me."

"This isn't about you and Lincoln anymore. It's about a murder. You need to go to the police," he says. "I told you before, this is bigger than you. You're *fifteen*, Jakub!"

But I shake my head. "Not the cops."

"Then what? Another piece of graffiti? You think that's going to help?" He points to the sketchbook in my hands. My breath catches in my throat.

Father Dom sees my hesitation. "Of course. You're fifteen. That *is* what you think will help, isn't it?"

I frown at him.

"That's not how it works. We aren't living in a comic book. You aren't a superhero."

Under the cover of night, I can believe in Morf, that he protects me. But sitting beside Father Dom, in a place where truths are told that cut to the quick, I feel small and helpless. Like a lost child.

I look at my lap. I gulp. The sketchbook is ridiculous. Fantasies for a different world. And my graffiti, the truths I thought I could shout, is a joke. I fucked up. No one is listening.

Someone bangs on the wooden front doors and I jump. Again, they pound, insistent. Father Dom sighs and slides to the end of the wooden pew. This late at night, only someone in desperate need of help would be on the church steps. Whoever it is hammers again.

I turn to the entrance as Father Dom slides the lock back and pulls open the door. I can hear voices, quick mutterings. Then Father Dom's voice booms out of the murky darkness. "Jakub. Come here."

Lincoln is on the church steps. His hood is up over his hat and I can't see his face. We stare at each other for a minute, or I stare at the spot where his eyes are supposed to be, and neither of us says anything.

"Do you want to come in, Lincoln?" Father Dom asks, breaking the silence.

But he shakes his head. "Went by your place," he says to me. "Your dad said you were here. Moving more books." He snorts. "You confessing your sins?" There's a bite to his voice, an edge I'm not used to hearing.

"I could listen to yours, too, if you wanted," Father Dom offers.

"How do you know I got any?"

Father Dom stays quiet and tilts his head at Lincoln. "We all sin, Lincoln."

Link shakes his head and snorts.

"Why are you here?" I ask.

He tips the brim of his hat up and his hood falls back. He presses his lips together and looks at me, like he's trying to decide something. "They saw your piece. The one of Lester. They know it's you."

"How?" I look at Link, dumbfounded. "No one knows I'm Morf. Unless —" I break off, the idea hard to believe. "Did you tell them?"

Link throws his head back in exasperation. "Wake the fuck up, Koob! Who else would care about Lester? Who else would do a piece for him?"

The silence between us is deafening. My face gets

red, flushed with panic. I thought I was untouchable, up there with my spray cans. "What are they going to do?"

Lincoln meets my eyes. "They sent me to find you. I'm supposed to bring you to them."

There's a sharp intake of breath from Father Dom. "Over my dead body," comes his thunderous reply.

"Fuck," I mutter, but my heart is pounding, cuz when I look at Link, I know he's not shitting me. I saw what they did to Lester. "What do I do?" I ask.

"Leave." There's no waver in his voice. "I'll go back, say I couldn't find you, but you have to go. Get out of the West End before someone sees you."

"And go where?" I choke on the words. "I don't have anywhere to go. Dad can't —" My voice cracks at the thought of Dad, of having to explain why we have to run.

Link shakes his head. "Why'd you get messed up in this shit, anyway?" He glares at me. "You shoulda stayed out of it."

"I tried."

Memories flood through my brain as I look at him. All the times we had each other's backs, me and Link against the world. I thought I was helping.

"What if I don't run? What if I go to the cops, tell them what I know. Say I found the body, saw some Red Bloodz running away?"

Father Dom nods. "Finally! One of you says something that makes sense."

"And then what? Henry lets me walk away? Think about it, Koob! He already knows I told you. What happens to me then, eh? You shoulda just stayed the fuck out of it! It wasn't your problem."

"It *was* my problem!" I fire back. "Lester's dead and I know who did it. What if it was you lying in the alley with your head bashed in? You think I wouldn't do something about it?"

"A piece of fucking graffiti isn't doing something about it!"

Father Dom yells, "Stop!" We stare at each other, tempers simmering. "Enough of this. I'm doing what I should have done in the first place. Both of you, inside." He holds the door open and I lean against it, watching his robes swish as he retreats, his footsteps rushed on the marble floor. I turn back to Lincoln, waiting for him to join me.

"I can't, man."

My stomach drops. He's bailing. He'd rather live as a murdering thug than do the right thing.

A car pulls up in front of the church, the kind with tinted windows and an engine that makes too much noise. Link turns, spinning to look at it. The driver and passenger side car doors open and two guys get out. "Father Dom," I call warningly. I listen for an answer, but there's just the echoing silence of the church.

My breath catches when I see it's Henry. The guy with him is scrawny compared to Lincoln's brother. Wiry, with hollowed out cheeks and eyes that dart between me and Link. The two of them open the back-seat doors. I think someone else will get out, but they just hang there, an ominous invitation. The car idles.

Henry walks slow, leisurely. *Run* beats in my head. But where? Where should I run? They're standing at the bottom of the stairs, twirling something in their hands, like batons. Lincoln is frozen in place, too.

Henry shakes his head, mockingly. "You don't follow directions so good, little brother." His voice, deep and gravelly, jolts me to my senses. The church doors shut as I take a step closer to Lincoln.

I see his chin quivering. His eyes don't leave the metal rod in Henry's hands — he keeps slapping it against his palm. The other guy glances at Henry and smirks. "Knew he was never Red Bloodz material."

"Run!" Link whispers to me between clenched teeth.

I look back at the church doors. A guy like Henry isn't going to let a place of worship get between him and a beating. I could bang, scream for Father Dom to open them, but that would put his life in danger. Henry won't want witnesses. I shudder at what that would mean.

Henry and the other guy come up the stairs slowly, the things in their hands spinning menacingly. When Henry gets close enough, he gives Lincoln a shove that sends him flying to the ground. "Jonny's right. Trying to warn the rat, eh?" He crouches down and gives Lincoln a long look. "You know what we do to rats, don't you?"

Jonny's eyes are trained on me. Up close, he's not much of a threat. Except for the weapon, I could take him. But against Henry I wouldn't stand a chance.

"Get him in the car," Henry says to Jonny. I search the street for a witness, someone I can shout out to, but it's empty.

Jonny takes a fake swing and I jump back. He gives a snort of laughter. "Not so tough without your spray cans, eh, you little faggot?" I don't say anything back to him. He looks at me with disgust, one lip curled up. "It's no fun if you don't fight back."

I narrow my eyes at him. Not fight back? My whole life I've been fighting. Maybe he doesn't think I look it, but I was raised in the West End, too. I know what it takes to survive here. If he thinks I'm not going to fight for my life, he's dead wrong.

LINCOLN

I hear something. A banging in the rear of the car.

Jonny gives Koob a grin, like how a wolf would before it attacks. "Hear that? Guess who we picked up on our way over?" Then, he turns to me. "Followed you to the Polack's place. More fight left in that old guy than I thought."

Mr. K? I look at Koob. His eyes get bigger than I've ever seen them and his mouth hangs open. "You got Mr. K?" I look at Henry and my guts churn.

"You got Mr. K?" He imitates me and spits in my face. "What the fuck do you care? He's not your family. Your family is right here." He points to his chest. "That kid is nothing to you, you hear me? Nothing! He's gotta learn not to mess with the Red Bloodz and you're the one who's gonna teach him."

They've got Mr. K. I blink trying to figure out why the hell Henry would do that, hurt a guy like Koob's dad. My mind's moving slow, processing all this. He moves to grab me and then I get it. They're gonna take us somewhere, an alley, back to the club house. Beat us, torture us, do whatever they want to teach us a lesson.

It's like Lester all over again.

Henry's grinning, one side of his mouth raised up, his eyes half-hooded, and then I feel it. A sudden rush of anger so intense it surprises me. It's hot and thick like lava and courses through my veins. The lava pumps into my heart and up to my head and it might explode.

The smile dies on Henry's mouth when Koob springs to life. In a second, he's wailing on Jonny, kicking and punching him to get to the car, to get to his dad.

"Dad!" Koob shouts, "Dad! I'm here!"

The blows catch Jonny by surprise. He puts his arm up to block them, the tire iron useless. But then Koob takes a breath, ready to run to his dad, and Jonny sees his chance. He raises the tire iron and brings it down hard on Koob's leg. Koob goes down, clutching it, but still yelling for Mr. K.

"Bring him to the alley," Henry says to Jonny and I *know* it's gonna be just like Lester. "Don't hurt him too bad. Not yet. This is Lincoln's boy. I want him to finish the job."

I guess it was always going to come to this. Henry making me choose between him and Koob.

Jonny gives Koob one more whack across the stomach. He gasps and moans and I look at Henry. "Either you do it, or you watch and we do the same thing to you."

I know he's telling the truth. It's how he made it through jail and how he's going to make the Red Bloodz into a gang that people respect and fear. And in the West End, that's the same thing.

I can still hear Mr. K's muffled shouts and hammering inside the trunk. He's calling Koob's name, over and over, at the top of his lungs. Koob's moaning on the steps. "Give it to me," I say and hold out my hand for the tire iron.

But Henry snorts and shakes his head. "Not yet." Jonny's dragging Koob to his feet and pulling him down the stairs. Koob's half-staggering, half-walking. Henry cracks his neck. He's like a hulk, standing beside me. I'm a powerless wimp.

Where's Skar now? I swallow the puke that rises in my throat. All the superhero talk me and Koob do when we're painting, sneaking around in the night, is bullshit. When it comes down to it and I have a chance to save someone, I turn into a weakling.

"I do know who my family is," I say. I keep my voice calm as my fingers wrap around the knife in my pocket. "Oh shit, cops!" I say, pointing.

When Henry turns, the knife comes out and the blade flicks open. It only takes a second. I lunge at Henry, holding the knife like a madman. I aim for the tattoo on his neck. But his body is all muscle and he's so much taller than me. He turns back before I'm close enough to plunge it in.

The tire iron comes fast and knocks me over. Stars flash in my eyes when my head hits the ground. "You fucker!" Henry shouts. I don't know where the knife is, but it's not in my hands. I search the pavement for it, trying to sit up. Henry stands on my hand, his boot crushing bones. I hear the crunch and then numbness. I scream with pain. "Compared to what I'm going to do to you and that little shit, I took it *easy* on Lester." His eyes flare like a mad dog, teeth bared.

And I know it's over. I can't fight against what was always going to happen. But I think about Dustin. I don't want him to know this is how it ended for me. And Koob. It'll be my fault if he and Mr. K die.

I can't let that happen.

Henry steps off my hand and hauls me to my feet. I see the knife. It's near my foot. Jonny and Koob aren't in front of the church anymore. They're around the back, in the alley. I just need one clear shot, one punch to distract him. My thoughts are clear now. I know what I have to do.

My fist comes quick under Henry's chin. His head jerks back and it's enough time for me to bend down and grab the knife. I spin around and jam it into a soft part on his stomach. The blade goes in quick and I let go, stumbling backward. Henry stares at me in shock, then takes a swing with the iron. The knife hasn't done enough damage. He's still fighting. But I'm free. I can run down the stairs quicker than him, leap down the last few and land on the sidewalk. From the corner of my eye, I see him stumble, holding his gut. He wobbles and goes down. Maybe punctured something, found its mark. I turn away. Koob, I think. Get to Koob.

I go to the alley. I see Jonny on the other side of a dumpster. He's got Koob up against the wall. Lying in the alley is a piece of wood, broken off from a pallet. I pick it up with my left hand. "Let my dad go," Koob begs. "Please."

"Jonny," I say, and when he turns to look, I whack him across the face with the board. It takes all my strength, but the hit wipes the smug look off his face. He staggers, shaking his head. My hand aches. The board falls to the ground and Koob sees his chance. He picks it up, gets between me and Jonny, and takes another swing at Jonny's head. He misses and hits Jonny's arm.

I turn around. The alley is empty. Henry hasn't followed me.

"Hit him in the head!" I shout at Koob, adrenaline coursing through me. Koob hesitates and Jonny comes at him, the tire iron like a baseball bat. I have nothing to lose, so I run at him, knocking him down. He tries to get up. Our spit and blood and sweat are all mixed together. I can see the stubble on his cheek, the way his hair grows in curly whorls around his face. He has a zit on his forehead. It's all there, registering in my brain, but all I'm thinking about is getting the tire iron away from him. My hand hurts too much to do any good; it hangs useless. Jonny's writhing under me, trying to get free. He whacks at my broken hand and the pain sends me reeling, falling off him.

And then Koob is there. He has the board in his hand and whacks Jonny's head with it. It's a sick thud and I've heard it before.

Jonny goes still.

The board clatters to the ground. The alley is silent except for our breathing and the far away wail of a siren.

JAKUB

I stumble back and hit the dumpster. Lincoln stands up, untangling his feet from Jonny's legs. He's shaking and he holds his hand, wincing with pain. "Is he — did I?" The words don't want to form on my tongue because I don't want to know the answer.

My head starts to clear and I remember my dad, locked in the trunk. I can see the car from the alley and head toward it, limping, my leg numb with pain. Link's beside me, then in front of me, running to it.

The car is still running, the rumbling engine drowning out the pound of blood in my brain. "Dad!" I yell. He's not banging on the trunk anymore. There's no noise at all. "Dad!" I shout again. Two police cars race through an intersection and screech to a stop, one behind the car, one in front.

An officer gets out of the first car. "Stop right there!" Link and I both freeze. His hands go up.

"Officer!" Father Dom's voice rings out. He's on the steps of the church and I wonder how much he saw. "Not them. They're the victims."

He doesn't acknowledge Father Dom. "Move to the sidewalk, both of you. Now!" the officer shouts. The other cops get out of the cars and fan out. Two come to us and one goes toward the church.

That's when I notice Henry. He's lying on the steps of the church. A dark stain has spread across his middle. "We're gonna need backup. And an ambulance," the officer says into his radio.

"My dad." Relief chokes my words. "He's in the trunk of the car." The cops look at each other. One stays with me and Link, and the other peers in the windows of the car. He pulls a glove out of his pocket and puts it on. He gets into the car and turns off the engine.

I close my eyes and pray. *Please let him be okay.*

The keys jangle in his hand as he walks around to the trunk. It creaks open and he holds the lid up with his gloved hand. "Make that two ambulances," he says into his radio.

I run, ignoring the pain in my leg and the officer guarding me. The cop by the car holds me back, but I fight past him, pushing his arm away. Dad's in the trunk, his face white. With fear or shock, I don't know. I don't even know if he's breathing.

"Dad?" I gasp.

"Jakub," he says weakly. My name a breath of air on his lips. One hand reaches up for mine. It's trembling and bloody. The knuckles scraped raw.

I grab it, but my knees buckle. I'm too weak to lift him out. "Dad," I sob, helpless.

Dad looks at me, his eyes pleading. "I thought they'd killed you," he says. "I thought — I thought I'd lost you —" he breaks off, his voice a hoarse, anguished whisper. I try to pull him out again and this time, I have the strength.

LINCOLN

The paramedics put Mr. K on a stretcher and wheel him to the ambulance. I watch it all from the sidewalk. I barely breathe when I see how pale Mr. K is, almost the same colour as the sheets. "You better come, too," one says to me, looking at my hand. Swollen knuckles hang limp and useless. "Get that checked out."

I shake my head, but then Koob looks my way, searching through all the cops and ambulance drivers to find me.

I duck. It's my brother who hurt his dad. My friggin' brother who wanted to kill him. How can I get in that ambulance beside him?

But the paramedic grabs my elbow and drags me toward the open doors. Koob moves away when he sees me coming, making room. I sit on a padded bench and watch as another guy in a blue outfit moves around the back of the ambulance, pulling things out of drawers and sticking a needle attached to a tube into Mr. K's arm.

"Is he gonna be okay?" I ask real quiet. Koob doesn't turn around, but his back stiffens, waiting to hear the answer.

"We'll be at the hospital soon. You can ask a doctor."

Feels like my chest is caving in watching the oxygen mask go over his face. Koob gets pushed out of the way and sits beside me so the paramedic can work. His face is worn out, like he's been awake for a week.

It's a long time before he says anything to me.

"I thought we were gonna die." Koob's voice shakes.

"Me too," I say, but it's just a whisper.

"I never should've done that piece," Koob says.

I want to say all the stuff I never should've done. Spill it so it leaks out of me. But that's not how it works. All that shit has to stay inside, buried deep somewhere so it doesn't hurt anyone else.

Henry's blood is on the sidewalk. Part of him staining the ground. Marking it.

Koob's breathing gets jumpy, and when I look over, he's got his eyes shut and his face screwed up, trying not to cry. I have to look away because my throat gets tight.

The siren wails as we pull into the street.

When we get to the hospital, they wheel Mr. K out first. Koob follows. I go a different way, to get my hand X-rayed. A cop takes me and we sit together in the waiting area.

"You know what happened to my brother?" I ask him. "The guy who got stabbed?" I can't help it. I have to know. But the cop gives me a tight-lipped shake of his head.

"We're going to take you to the police station after your hand gets looked at. Who should we call to meet you?"

I think about the phone ringing at my house. How pissed Mom will be when it wakes her. She might not even answer it. Might just take it off the hook, worried it'll wake Dad or Dustin. I shrug at the cop. "We can't question you unless there's someone present," he says.

I give him the number and wonder how I'm gonna explain all this shit to Mom. What will she do when she finds out about Henry? That I'm the one who stabbed him? My foot starts jittering and I take a shaky breath. The lump in my throat gets bigger, harder to hide. I feel tears burning behind my eyes.

"You sure you can't find out about my brother?" I ask again. My voice cracks. I'm trying to keep it together.

"Sorry," the cop says and shakes his head.

"Lincoln Bear?" A nurse in a pale purple outfit calls my name. She's young and pretty, and I wish I was following her for a different reason. "What happened?" she asks, glancing at my hand.

"Got in a fight," I say. But she looks at the cop behind me and looks back at me.

"Okay. We'll get it fixed up for you." Her voice is real gentle and I want to curl up in a corner with the kindness of it. I hold my mouth tight, glad she's not asking any more questions.

When we get to the police station, Mom's already there. She's got on a T-shirt and old sweatpants and that stupid track jacket of Henry's. She stands up when she sees me. Her eyes go to the bandage on my hand. "You okay?" she says.

I nod. Three broken bones, the doctor said, but small ones. No point in casting it. As long as I don't move it, they should heal.

"This way." The officer opens a door to a room. It's not like the movies; there's no two-way glass. Just a window with steel mesh on the other side of it and blinds pulled halfway down. It's still dark out. Night's on the other side of the window.

A new cop comes in, a woman, and asks me a bunch of questions. She writes my answers down on a pad of paper. The whole time, I feel Mom's eyes on me and I wish they'd never called her. "You arresting him?" she asks, suspiciously.

"No, just asking questions. Trying to find out what happened. So," she turns to me, "Why were you at the church?"

I peek at Mom. She narrows her eyes at me. There's no way to tell the story without talking about Lester. I stall.

The cop taps her pen on the desk.

"To get Koob."

"Why?"

"Cuz."

She puts her pen down, like she's prepared to be here for a while, wait me out. "Were the two of you going somewhere? Meeting someone?"

I blink. Not once, lots. I can't help it. Mom leans in and I can hear her breathing. "Henry told me to find him."

It goes on like this for a while. It's tiring. My hand's on fire, the pain's intense even though they gave me T-3's at the hospital. I want to go to sleep. I don't know what time it is, but the night sky outside is getting lighter. "When your brother showed up, you got into a fight. What was it about?"

"He wanted to hurt Koob."

"You haven't told me why. Why did he want to hurt your friend?"

I've been dancing around it all night. The only way I'm getting out of here is if I tell her. When I look at her face, I think she already knows. Koob probably told her, spilled everything. I try to wiggle my fingers under the bandages, but pains stabs through my hand.

"Cuz Koob found out about Lester."

"Who's Lester?"

"He lived in Koob's building." I pause, not sure if I can do it, but the words are right there. "Henry killed him." It's like all the air gets sucked out of the room when I say those words. Mom makes a choking noise beside me.

"Shut up," she hisses. Her eyes dart to the cop.

But I shake my head at her. They probably know everything, anyway. Or maybe they saw Koob's piece, same as Henry did, and are fishing for information. It doesn't matter. I'm dead either way. "Screw it," I mutter under my breath. No point in stopping now.

I trace the events back to the beginning, like following a vein in my arm, back to the first meeting at the fast food place with Henry and his plans for stealing cars. I'm done protecting the Red Bloodz, done playing by their rules. I'm out of the game. It never made sense to me, anyway.

I start to shake when I tell her about what we did to Lester in the alley. She leans across the desk, frowning.

"And you left him there?"

I nod.

"Your brother, Henry, he was the one to deliver the final blow. The one you think killed him?"

I nod again. Puke rises in my throat, but I swallow it down. I stare at my hands. Another cop comes in the room and calls the woman cop out. Her chair scrapes the floor when she leaves.

I look at Mom when she's gone. She's fiddling with the strap of her purse, but a tear rolls down her cheek and lands on the T-shirt. I wonder if she's gonna say anything, but she doesn't. Just wipes her cheek and sniffles.

When the cop comes back in, she sits down and looks at me. There's another cop behind her, a tall guy in a uniform. "Your brother's dead, Lincoln." She sighs. "I'm charging you for the murder of Henry Bear," she says.

Mom's purse falls to the floor, stuff clatters out. She doesn't pick it up, just stares at the cop, shaking her head. "No," she says. "He told you what happened! Weren't you listening?" She stretches her arm across my chest, keeping them away. "Henry would have killed him!"

The cop keeps talking. "And for the assault of Lester McFarlane. For car theft and conspiracy to commit —" but her words are drowned out by Mom's cries and the pounding in my head.

JAKUB

I visit Link once a week. I did the math when he got sentenced. Figured out how many Saturday afternoon visits we'd have before his three-year sentence was up. Five down, one hundred-fifty-one to go.

The room at the Youth Correction Centre is blank. Nothing in it but a table and some chairs. The door clicks open. Link walks in, and the door shuts after him. There's a guard outside, peering in through the window.

He cut his hair for court, but it's grown out again, shaggy around his ears. Without a baseball hat on, I can see his whole face. How much he looks like Henry.

"Hey," he says, and holds his fist up for a bump.

"Hey, man." I grin bigger than I mean to, trying to cover up how hard it is to see him like this. There's so much I want to say, but not here. Not now.

"Father Dom came by yesterday. Said you start at your new school this week," Link says.

"Should be good. Closer to home." It's less high-end than St. Bart's, but Father Dom pleaded my case with Father O'Shea, and together they got me in. The school is called Holy Redeemer Academy, so I guess they kind of had to take me. If anyone is looking for redemption, it's me. I got community service for helping Link steal the car, but Jonny survived the blow to the head I gave him. Lucky for me.

Henry's death and the raid on the chop shop and the clubhouse left the Red Bloodz in tatters. All the guys went away for something. Link would be out first. His confession helped the cops nail the others, but the other gang members don't know that. The threat of retribution hangs heavy over him. He'll spend the rest of his life looking over his shoulder. Even when it's just the two of us, he checks the exits. His eyes are watchful, darting to the door, at the windows. He doesn't sleep much; there's dark circles under his eyes. He's talked about the guilt that weighs on him. I see it in his shuffling walk. Head bowed, shoulders slumped. Each time I visit, I hope for a smile, a flicker of the Lincoln I knew before.

It's almost time for me to go when Link leans across the table and stares at me. His scar shines pink, high-lighted by the fluorescent lights. "I been doing a lot of thinking, you know. About how things got like this. How I ended up here."

He pulls a paper out of the pocket of his overalls. He unfolds it slowly and lays it on the table in front of me. "I thought maybe you could do something to remember Lester. I know he never had a funeral or nothing." The sketch is of Lester's face. Even with his messed-up hand, it's the best thing he's ever done.

He's blinking, waiting for my reaction. I stare at it for a long moment. "It's good, Link. Really good."

His Adam's apple bobs when he swallows. His eyes get wet and I wish there was something I could do or say to make it easier for him. To let him know I wish things were different.

The guard outside raps on the door. Our time is up. "Stay in the room, Lincoln. You have another visitor," he says. Link's face lights up and he looks at me, expectantly.

I shake my head. It's not Dad. Every week, Link asks about him, desperate to see him. Dad says he might be ready one day, but not yet. He thought he was going to die in that trunk. He thought they'd killed me. He's not a heavy sleeper anymore; his nightmares keep us both awake.

"Guess I'll get going." I slide the paper back to him.

But he shakes his head. "Keep it. Take a picture when you throw it up, okay?"

I fold it and put it in my pocket. My heart's heavy.

He holds his fist up for a bump. I hesitate. I want to give him more, but there isn't anything else. Our fists collide.

On my way out, I pass Dustin and Lincoln's mom. Dustin's jumping up and down, so excited to see Lincoln. I look back through the glass window on the door and watch for a minute.

Dustin races into the room and jumps into Lincoln's arms. The kid clutches him around the neck and Link picks him up, holding him close. They don't let go of each other for a long time.

Dad's waiting outside for me on a bench. He stands up when he sees me coming, resting on the cane he finally agreed to use. "How was it?" he asks.

I pull out Lincoln's sketch of Lester and hand it to Dad. The paper trembles in his hand when he looks at it, gripping his cane tighter. There are tears in his eyes when he gives it back to me.

"He doesn't belong in there," I say, my voice thick. He was more my brother than Henry's, but it was Henry who claimed him, who left his mark on him. Another scar Link would carry for the rest of his life.

There's nothing Dad can say. Regret runs deep in me; he sees how it's etched into my face and in the pages of my sketchbook.

As we walk home, Dad leans on me. His broken body and twisted leg imperfect, but strong enough to carry me through times like these. To lead me to a better place.

ACKNOWLEDGEMENTS

Thank you to Sheldon Nelson and Cindy Kochanski for their thoughtful and insightful comments, and to my agent, Harry Endrulat, for his support and advice. Thank you Val and Ritchie Miller for answering my questions related to public safety. Some of the questions probably made them wonder about what I was doing in my spare time. ("So, let's say I'm caught tagging a building …") Thank you to Jamie Gatta, who breathed life into Morf and Skar's artwork.

Thank you to the team at Dundurn Press: Carrie Gleason for her belief in the book; Margaret Bryant and Jaclyn Hodsdon for ensuring that it finds its way into the world; Cheryl Hawley and Catherine Dorton for making the process smooth and the writing better; Jennifer Gallinger for the design; and Laura Boyle for creating the cover.

Much appreciation to the Winnipeg Arts Council for providing generous support during the editing and revision of the manuscript.

A special thank you to McNally Robinson Booksellers and their amazing staff. Winnipeggers are lucky to have an independent bookstore that champions local authors.

Finally, thank you, as always, to my friends and family for their ongoing support.